THE RYZEN SAGA

Book One

The New Recruit

J.D. Warburton

The Ryzen Saga by J.D. Warburton

ISBN 978-1-952027-06-2 (Paperback)
ISBN 978-1-952027-11-6 (Hardback)

This book is written to provide information and motivation to readers. Its purpose is not to render any type of psychological, legal, or professional advice of any kind. The content is the sole opinion and expression of the author, and not necessarily that of the publisher.

Printed in the United States of America.
New Leaf Media, LLC
470 W Broad St #1276
Columbus, OH 43215
www.thenewleafmedia.com

Time devours all things.
All that is created will be destroyed.

Time is insurmountable,
Change is inevitable,
Destruction is transformation;
Time kills all that are born.

Solid mountains shake to the ground,
Mighty oceans swallow the land;
Time is awake while all else sleeps.

Only knowledge will see the new day.

From the Vidura of the Makarish

Prologue

Long ago, ten thousand years before the Roman Empire cast its shadow over the lands, there were civilizations all around the earth. They were not the first civilization on the globe, but they had restored some of the old learning, and there were a few who knew how to use that knowledge to fly above the cities and plains, to soar above mountains and through the oceans even as their contemporaries voyaged in reed boats and wooden ships with brightly colored sails. These few were the best of the best, the guardians of the old learning. They were called the Ryzen, and this is the story of one of their order.

Chapter 1

"Knowledge is the most important thing. Without it one cannot achieve one's goal; yet, if it is not translated into action, it becomes useless."

~ Tome of the Ryzen

Last Day of Spring

Undergraduate Halls, Maga Vihar

Tambak Citadel, Timur Laut continent

Maz sauntered down the hallway of the Maga Vihar, the foremost place of learning in the Citadel, trying to look casual and failing miserably. His student tunic worn over dark green trousers was sparkling white, having been recently cleaned; he was tall and coppery-bronze, and his long, wavy dark hair was confined in a thick tail at the nape of his neck, drawing the favorable attention of the female students as he walked by. He couldn't suppress the grin on his face or the bounce in his step as he approached the office of the Ryzen liaison, where he was sure his application would be accepted.

The Ryzen were the best of the best. They were the keepers of ancient knowledge, the guardians of wisdom. They were the ones the Grandmothers trusted to protect the people of Timur Laut from their enemies. They were the strongest, and the bravest, and the smartest people in the entire world, and Maz had wanted to be a Ryzen for as long as he could remember. Finally, after so many years of waiting to be old enough, today he passed the one and a half dozen years needed to be considered a young adult, twelve plus six years, and today he was taking that first step. His life was about to truly begin.

He pushed the door open and entered the room. It was airy and open, with very little in the way of furnishings; a couple of high tables, stools, shelves with books, and very little else. A man sat at the table nearest to the door, facing the entrance. He wore the traditional Ryzen uniform, with a blue-trimmed vest over a gray tunic and long trousers. His hair was clubbed back into a short, efficient braid. Although some Ryzen came from other lands, this man was obviously from Timur Laut, just like Maz, with copper skin, dark hair and eyes, and clan tattoos. He looked at Maz, raising an eyebrow inquisitively.

"Good day, student. How may the Ryzen serve you?"

"Good day, Ryzen. I want to join up!"

"Really? Why?"

Maz stared at him. "Because the Ryzen are the best! I've wanted to be a Ryzen all my life! My uncle was a Ryzen, and I've always looked up to him. He's a hero. That's how I know the Ryzen are the best."

The man smiled. "I know the Ryzen are the best. I want to know why you think you are good enough to join the Ryzen."

Maz smiled back. This was familiar ground.

"I just finished my Academy course with highest honors. I've won awards in every sport I ever tried. I know I can do well in pretty much everything. That's why."

The smile became broader. "Youngling, you would never make it as a Ryzen. Go home and play with your toys. The Ryzen aren't taking in children."

Maz was stunned. He hadn't expected anything but a warm welcome. His uncle had been a Ryzen, and he'd just assumed he would be able to apply when he finished the Academy.

"I'm not a child! I'm one and one-half dozen years old, and I completed the Academy. I want to join!"

The Ryzen stood and walked over to him. He was half a hand taller, but not as broad as Maz. He put a hand on his shoulder, as a kind uncle or teacher might.

"Little mouse, you can't always have what you want. Some things need to be earned. Apparently you still need to learn that. As I said, go home to your mother." He patted Maz on the cheek.

"Come back when you need to shave your chin hairs."

Maz turned and walked out, furious. How could this happen? How was it even possible? The Ryzen wanted the best, and he was certainly the best. He did well in everything he tried. They didn't know who they were refusing. Hadn't he won the spring boat races by three lengths? And that Ryzen treated him like a child! He walked aimlessly, fuming. This wasn't right. How could they just turn him away without even giving him a chance?

He had walked aimlessly around the city for half an hour before he found himself back in front of the Ryzen office. He had walked in circles without noticing. His frustration was high. Taking a deep breath, he went back into the office, determined to be heard.

"Back again so soon, Mouse?"

"I want to join the Ryzen." Maz glared at the man.

"You said that. Nothing has changed."

"Isn't there a test I can take? Some way I can prove myself?"

"Of course there is. It's for men and women who want to join the Ryzen. You won't pass it, though. It's very difficult." The man was still smiling.

"I'll pass it. Just give it to me. I want to take it."

"Think carefully, now. There's a written test and a physical performance test. They're both difficult. Are you sure you want to try?"

"Yes. I want to try. I'll show you I can do it."

"All right, then. Start with the written test. Remember to read the entire test before you start."

He handed Maz a long sheet of real paper, such as was used at the Academy for examinations; a square glass for enlarging small writing; a fine brush; a square of pressed ink; and a wet sponge in a bowl—the standard student writing kit. Maz sat at the other table and set out the implements, as he would do in class. The Ryzen brought him a book bound with wooden covers. It looked as if it had seen years of use.

"Put your name on the top of the paper. Read through the entire test before you begin. Answer questions one through four dozen, in characters that are neat and easy to read. No sloppy angles. Do you understand, Mouse?"

"It's Maz, not Mouse."

"That's what I said. When you've completed the written portion, I'll start you on the physical part."

Maz hurried through the questions as quickly as he could without making his writing sloppy. He didn't need to read them all first, just started right in with the first question and continued on. They were simple questions; basic mathematics, simple history of Timur Laut, questions about legends of the past, and about the geography of their continent and the Western Islands. A few questions about the seasons, the stars, and types of rock. There were four dozen questions, as he had been told, and some more words at the end of the book in very small characters. He didn't bother to read those, even with the glass attached to the book that helped make small characters easier to read. That was for old people, and the questions were the important part. He answered every one, and he was sure he had done well when he handed the form to the Ryzen.

"So soon?"

"It wasn't hard."

"Did you read the last page?"

Maz was confused. "Last page?"

"Yes, the last page in the book. Did you read it?"

"I think I read everything. I'm pretty sure I did. Except the really small characters."

"Those characters at the end? Well, no matter. Let's get on to the physical test. Come out to the yard behind the building, and we'll get started."

Still confused, Maz found himself wishing he had taken the trouble to read the last page, even if he needed the enlarging glass. He stepped outside into a huge open yard to see a running track around the perimeter, just inside a low stone wall, with a stone-lined swimming pond in the center and a rock-embedded climbing wall on one side. Around the pool were familiar structures for a training circuit; ropes for swinging across a huge frame, a tall tree without low branches that was positioned for climbing, and all the other things used to train athletes. He had used this type of circuit when preparing for the spring boat race, as well as for regular fitness.

The Ryzen handed him a wooden tablet. On it were written the names of the training structures in the circuit, in order, including the track and the pond. He also had a glass timer, filled with colored sand that filtered from one section to the other.

"Do all the things on this list in this order. Do not change the order or skip anything. Run the circuit a full hand of times. You must finish before the time runs out. This is important. Be sure to do your best and show me what you've got. Remember, do your best."

Maz grinned. This would be easy. He had run this type of course dozens of times! The Ryzen turned the timer, and Maz stripped to his loincloth and started. He took a fairly easy pace the first time, and based on how much sand was left, figured out how to pace himself to complete the fifth circuit in the allotted time.

It wasn't difficult, and he found it enjoyable. He liked running, climbing, and swimming, and the variation from swinging across the space on ropes to climbing the tree, climbing a rock-embedded wall, and he found that the other challenges on the circuit were almost a relief after weeks of studying for the final examinations. He timed it perfectly, and he completed the fifth circuit and reported back to the Ryzen just a few heartbeats before the last grain of sand fell.

The Ryzen looked at him. He did not look happy.

"Well, Mouse, you completed it in the time allotted. Now, go and clean up, put your tunic and trousers back on. and meet me back in the office."

Maz did as he ordered, wondering why the Ryzen didn't seem pleased. He cleaned up at the washing station, dried off and put on his clothes. Then he went back into the office.

"How did I do? I passed, right? I can join the Ryzen and start training?"

The Ryzen looked at him, and Maz's heart sank. He could tell by that look what was coming.

"No, Mouse, you didn't pass."

"What? How can that be?"

"The first thing a Ryzen recruit must do is follow instructions. You didn't do that. That's why you failed."

"What instructions? I did everything you told me!"

"Did you read every word of the test before you began?"

"Of course! Well…most of them, anyway." Maz remembered the small characters at the end of the book.

"Don't lie to a Ryzen, Mouse."

"I'm not lying! I …read all the questions. I just didn't read the end part."

"I know, because the end part instructed you to write your name on the paper, and then put it on the table in front of you without answering any questions."

"What? But…that's not fair."

"A recruit must be able to follow instructions. That's the beginning of wisdom. If you can't take instruction, you can't learn. If you can't learn, there's no point in going forward."

Maz felt tears begin to well up behind his eyes. He knew he was wrong. He had been told to read everything. He had been given the opportunity, and he let it slip through his grasp.

"What about the physical part? Did I pass that?"

"What was my instruction to you? Did I not tell you to do your best, to show me your top performance?"

"Yes, sir, you did."

"Did you give me your top performance?"

Maz was silent for a moment. "I made it in the time allotted, sir."

"Could you have done it faster?"

Maz had nothing to say. Of course he could have gone faster, and the Ryzen knew it. He shook his head.

"I could have done better, sir. But I thought it was good enough to meet the qualifications."

"What's your uncle's name? The one who is a Ryzen?"

"CreeVa Kau. Why?"

The Ryzen didn't answer. He appeared lost in thought for a moment. Then he took a deep breath, as if he had made a decision.

"A Ryzen has to be able to follow instructions. Only then will you know when it is good to diverge from them. Look, Mouse, you seem like a good boy. If you can find a Ryzen who is willing to train you, you may present yourself for the open test at dawn on the day of the fall equinox. Be at the gate to the Citadel exactly at sunrise, with a Ryzen teacher at your side. That's all the advice I can give you. Now go find some cheese, Mouse. You look like you need a meal."

Chapter 2

"Reflect on yourself and develop a desire to rise above your ideals and be more than you imagine; this can only be attained through disciplining yourself through your thoughts, words, and deeds."

From the Tome of the Ryzen

Sky and Stars Building, Maga Vihar

Maz climbed the steps to his father's laboratory. Not waiting for a response to his knock on the door, he opened it and entered, looking around for his father.

Tamu Kau was a tall and slender man, lacking his son's bulk but surpassing him by a finger's width in height. His straight, dark hair with a dusting of gray at the temples was tied in a single braid at the back of the neck, not as wild as his son's style, and his brown eyes squinted a bit as he peered at the young man entering his lab. He absentmindedly wiped his hands on his red tunic before reaching out to grip Maz' forearms in greeting.

"Mazkawa! Done with your testing already?"

"Yes, Pa! I passed! Highest honors!" Maz returned the grip, noticing how thin his father's arms were getting. Tamu wasn't eating properly these days, and wasn't taking time for strength training—a lapse he would never allow in his children. The current research project, whatever it was, consumed the dedicated Senhan's time and energy.

Tamu was the Diviga Rishi, the senior Senhan or Professor of the Study of Stars and Skies there at the Maga Vihar, the foremost center of learning in all the lands. In his youth, he had improved the design of the far-seer that brought the stars within the view of scholars, refining the device and extending its capabilities. He had mapped the stars more precisely than anyone in Timur Laut had done since the times of the ancients, earning the gratitude of sea voyagers as well as land explorers and Ryzen pilots across the land. Wayfinding had become more exact since Tamu Kau first gazed at the stars, and his students went on to do great things with the knowledge he gained from his research.

"Highest honors, eh? Wonderful, wonderful! We should celebrate! Especially since this is your birth anniversary!"

"How about a nice meal at the falu pau down the street in Maga Vihar Square? The one that serves unlimited bread and fruit with every meal? And those wonderful prasava pies?" Maz wasn't that hungry, but he wanted to get his father to eat. He knew Tamu was skipping meals and forgetting to eat, being so immersed in his research. This would be a way to get something in his stomach. Tamu liked prasava pies. The slightly tart fruit in a flaky, sweet crust could always tempt him away from his studies.

"That sounds good, son. Your mother is still out in the field, finishing up training the new group of students in their healer training program. I'm getting tired of the food here. The students who operate it know their teachers; they apparently think we don't care about what we eat, so they don't take time to prepare the food as well as other places, and they don't have prasava pies. Let's go! You can tell me all about your tests while we eat."

The absent-minded Senhan grabbed his black, wide-sleeved formal robe from a hook on the wall, slipped it over his shoulders, grabbed his red, feathered, round hat, and was ready to go.

Maz smiled happily as he and his father left the laboratory. He smoothed his dark, curly hair and re-tied the band confining it at the back of his neck. He was still dressed in the white student tunic he had worn for his tests, but that didn't matter. Lots of other students would be out celebrating test results and the end of the academic term. No one would think twice about his casual attire.

Maz and Tamu walked briskly through the halls of the Maga Vihar, nodding and smiling as they passed people they knew, students and senhani. As they emerged from the Sky and Stars Studies building into the bright sunlight, a cheerful voice hailed them.

"Pa! Maz! Just in time!" Maz turned to see his older brother Draq approach, easily recognizable in his bright orange uniform with the quilted short jacket worn by all the technical crew of the vimana force. It was different from the Ryzen vests, being shorter and brightly colored. Maz wondered if he should think about a career in the defense forces, after all. Maybe he should give up his dream.

"Draq! How nice! Both my sons together! Will you join us for dinner?"

"Sure, Pa! With Ma out of town and Tahari busy with her young students' final day celebration, there's no one at home. I'd starve! The food back at the landing field is truly terrible."

"Draq! Good to see you!" Maz and his brother clasped forearms, grinning happily. They hadn't seen each other in months. Draq was trained as a Vatiga Rishi, an expert in metals and minerals, and had just been awarded a place on a Sikka Manu. He currently worked in the wailu kile foundry, refining and processing the valuable ore that powered the flying Vimana; the larger, three-person Sikka Manu; and the Ichak, the staffs the elite Ryzen carried. He enjoyed the work, but had hoped to join the crews who traveled on the exotic Sikka Manu to the mines and brought back the raw ore; that had been a dream of his for years. That new assignment would begin soon, and he was looking forward to talking with his family about it. Between his regular shift and his extra training, plus his blade-making hobby, he'd been too busy lately to spend much time with his family.

Draq was shorter than his father or brother, but not by much. His face was rounder, his smile wider, and his dark braid, worn at the top of his head, military style, got noticed by the ladies wherever he went. He was five years older than Maz, and when they were young Maz idolized his big brother and followed him everywhere. He still idolized him, but had long since stopped being a little follower, enjoying his own popularity on campus as big brother went off to the military.

The three men continued on to the falu pau, reaching it just before the dinner rush. It was one of the better eating places in the city, operated by farmers and ranchers who worked there as part of their obligation to the Maga Vihar when family members pursued their studies. Instead of the student-run facilities in the various schools and residence halls, this was operated by the people who produced the food, and they were proud of what they offered.

After only a short wait, they were seated at a table and the server brought cups of water and a basket of fresh, crusty bread. Maz was delighted. He was always hungry, and the idea of unlimited bread sounded wonderful. He broke a piece off one of the flat loaves and dipped it in the seasoned nut oil that was already waiting in small, shallow dishes on the table.

Draq didn't wait. "So tell us about your tests! How did you do?"

"Great," Maz said around a mouthful of bread. He continued to eat while he told them about his performance on his tests. History, natural science, astronomy, computation, engineering and architecture; he excelled in every subject.

"That sounds great," his father said. "But I don't understand. You said you missed one question in computation, and I think you said you went over your time?"

"That's right! One computation error, plus I had a wrong date for the beginning of the Great War, and fifteen seconds too long on my speech. That's all! Isn't that great?"

Tamu smiled. "That was the preliminary result, right? You corrected those and redid the exams for a perfect score?"

Maz frowned. "Uh, no, Pa. I think highest honors are pretty good. There isn't any higher level. Sure, they said I could redo the things I missed, but why? There's no benefit to doing that."

His father and brother looked at each other. Then Draq spoke.

"Maz, that would be great for most people. But I thought you wanted to try for the Ryzen?"

He shrugged his shoulders. "I did. But they don't want me, so it doesn't matter anymore. Besides, highest honors ought to be good enough!" He tried to look as if he didn't care, but it didn't work.

"Something is bothering you, son. You say it went well, but your eyes tell a different story," said Tamu.

"Pa, I went to the Ryzen training office and asked to apply. They said no. I went back and asked again, and they gave me some tests. I failed them. I still don't completely understand why." He told them what happened, in every detail.

"Maz, I failed the Ryzen assessment." Draq spoke softly, almost whispering. "It's been five years, but it still bothers me. And it was the right outcome. I've done well in the defense forces. The vimana program is excellent. But some of my colleagues in the force are Ryzen, and I see the difference."

"I didn't know you applied to join the Ryzen," Maz said. This was astonishing. Being one of the elite group of warriors was his lifelong dream. He had no idea his brother had also shared that dream.

"Yeah, well, I didn't talk about it. I wasn't prepared. I should have told Pa I was thinking about it. It might have made a difference. If we had spoken about it, you might have done things differently and had better success. I know I wish I had listened to the advice I got."

"Why? What would you have done differently? I didn't realize that school scores were so important!" Maz heard the stress in his own voice and breathed slowly, trying to calm himself.

"It's not the school scores, it's deeper than that. I've known Ryzen who didn't have highest honors, or even high honors, Maz. They passed the Ryzen assessments. It's hard to explain."

"What is it, Draq? What am I missing?"

"Mazkawa," said Tamu, using his full name as always, "my brother, your uncle Cree, is a Ryzen. After the war he took a leave of absence to do farming and spend time with his children. But I always knew he was different. He has something. I haven't been sure if you just didn't have it, or if you would grow into it. I'm still not sure, but something you said today concerns me."

Stunned, Maz stared at them. "What is it? What don't I have?" He felt his dreams crumbling around him.

"I don't have a word for it," said Draq, "but I know what it looks like. I've never heard a Ryzen do anything but his or her absolute best. You declined fixing your errors because the result was good enough... but it wasn't your best, Maz. You skipped reading the written test because it was a bother to use the glass. You paced yourself in the physical test because you thought it was all right to just make the minimum. That wasn't your best. It was your second best. And a Ryzen never gives second best. It's nothing but the best."

"It's a state of mind, son. It's not scores. It's not how high you jump or how fast you run. It's what you give of yourself. It's what you give of your body, your mind, your spirit." Tamu reached out and touched him on the chest, right over his heart.

"If you want, son, you can go to the University. I reserved a place for you when you were born. You could study whatever field you like. You'll do well, and you'll have a good life."

"But I won't be a Ryzen!" Maz said, in a pained whisper.

"Do you want that? Do you really, really want it?"

Maz thought for a moment. "Yes, Pa, I do. I really do. I want it more than anything. What can I do?"

"What are you willing to do?" his father asked.

"Whatever it takes. Anything. Everything."

His father's response surprised him. "I think you need to spend the summer on the farm with your uncle Cree."

"Uncle Cree? Why? I mean, I know he's a Ryzen, but he's been on a farm for thirty years. He's retired, right?"

"Not at all, son. He merely changed his occupation. I don't believe you've heard this part of his story. After the war, he left the defense forces because he believed his talents were no longer needed there in peacetime. Others could do the job of peacetime defense, but very few could bring a community to life."

"I haven't heard this either, Father. Will you tell us?" Draq asked. They knew he was interested in restoring the crafts of earlier times, some of the methods that had been lost over the years. His latest interest was in forging iron tools with a method that mixed other ores to make a stronger metal. He enjoyed making knives and other hand tools, and often made gifts to his family of his creations.

"Yes, please." said Maz.

"Of course. You see, the region of Banua Zalagi was almost deserted. There is rich farmland, but the few townships in the region were seriously damaged in the war. Before the conflict, this agricultural region had become largely residential, as it changed from farmland and ranches to a region of wealthy people's vacation homes and a haven for retirees. That reputation is probably why you thought your uncle had retired, but it's not true.

"After the war, many of the little communities and some of the primitive tribal areas in the region, now made up of fashionable homes with flower gardens and a few kitchen gardens, were deserted. The residents had mostly lost their wealth in the war and moved back to the large cities of the surrounding provinces. Many young people died in the war, leaving old people and children. Banua Zalagi had no trade, no commerce, no industry. Today, the region produces most of the exotic food served in the cities, from an organized farming system, livestock ranchers, and a network of independent hunters who provide all the boar and aurochs the dinner houses and inns can use. The people of Banua Zalagi are wealthy again, but it is through their own hard work. Their children and grandchildren have a good future, thanks to CreeVa Kau."

"Uncle Cree? How did he do that?" Maz was astonished. He had thought of his uncle as a retired soldier, sipping mead and boring everyone with war stories.

"He gave them the Ryzen vision. They began to work with all their faculties, putting everything within them into whatever they did. They farmed every inch of arable land, raised livestock in byres and barns, hunted the wild boar and fearsome aurochs in the forests, and sold to the markets in the cities. Everyone was fairly paid what was honestly earned, and they prospered—not just financially, but in good health and thriving, vibrant families and communities.

"So did he—what? Encourage them?"

"Perhaps, in part, but mainly he showed them how to make the most of what they had. He showed them how to think like a Ryzen. If a farmer had a few hectares of land, he showed him how to get maximum yield. If a family had a cottage in the woods with only a small kitchen garden, he showed them how that garden, plus a few ground birds and goats, could feed their family while the less skilled members hunted boar in the woods and learned to sell the meat to inns and chop houses. Those with book talent kept accounts, for a fee; widows with large, empty houses rented rooms and sold prepared meals with food from their gardens. Every person began to see possibilities. He had a thousand ideas, and people took them and applied them. They honor him for it. He is Craftmaster for the region, respected in every corner. He used to come to the Gathering at the Maga Vihar every year, and the Crafts all talk about the Banua phenomenon. Many have tried, but to this day no one has been able to duplicate his success. Now his underlings represent him at the Gathering, and he stays home teaching his grandchildren. Banua Zalagi is the wealthiest region on the continent. They have no poor people, because the disabled are well cared for by their families or by the community, and every able bodied person is working up to his or her potential. No one settles for what's good enough; it must be excellence, because they can imagine nothing else."

The server brought them food, and they began eating. It was a savory stew of aurochs meat with maize and peppers, served with more of the tasty bread, and followed with Tamu's favorite prasava pie. There was a dark brewed ale, fragrant with yeast, to wash it down with. Maz had a good appetite and wasted not a scrap of the delicious meal. He made a point of urging Tamu to eat more, and Draq joined in.

"He's right, Pa. You haven't been eating well. Doesn't the senhani's falu pau at the Maga Vihar feed you? I know Ma has been gone a lot, but you mustn't forget to eat!"

"I know, boys. I just get busy and don't think of it most days. I've been working on something that's really occupying my mind."

"Can you talk about it?" asked Maz.

"Oh, yes. It isn't secret or anything. It's just... well... inconclusive, I should say. That's what's troubling. I'm seeing things I've never seen in the northern sky, and I've searched the records for any mention of a similar phenomenon in the past. I've gone as far back as the time of Lin the Musician and there's nothing like it."

"That's, what, two dozen dozens squared of years ago?" Maz said.

"That's close. Nineteen dozens squared and a hand. Long enough to think this is no ordinary pattern of stars. I think it's changing position, and that shouldn't be possible!"

"Is this something you're seeing with the new lens in the star viewer, Pa?"

"Yes, Draq. It's a wonderful invention! It might be that this oddity has always been in the sky and we simply lacked the ability to see it."

"I understand that very well. Since I've been working as a Vatiga Rishi, I've been amazed at how new inventions and ideas can change the way we see things. Just being up in the air, even as a passenger, gives a different perspective of things. It may be something you'll understand after studying it for a while. But you shouldn't forget to eat!" Draq said, laughing as he handed his father another piece of bread.

They finished eating, and Draq insisted on paying, handing the server a strip of beaded cloth and waving magnanimously at him to keep the change when offered a few beads in return.

"It's my treat," he insisted. "A Vatiga Rishi on a Sikka Manu gets more than twice what a foundry tech earns. I've even sold some of my knives, although I don't do it for the money. Matter of fact, Maz, I'm just about finished with a knife for your name day, which I remembered is coming up on the equinox, because your birth anniversary is right about this time, right? My mark will be on it, and I'm making a sheath with your name inscribed in the leather. I'm working with the metal pattern, a layered method that's completely new. It's just like this one," he said, taking it out and showing it to Maz. It was a beautiful knife with a complicated pattern forged right into the metal.

"That's a beautiful knife!" Maz said, admiring it.

"And it was made by a professional knife maker, no less. Me!! I'm rich these days!"

"Until you find a wife, son. Then it won't seem like much at all!"

"Truth, Pa! But the girl I have my eye on earns plenty on her own; she's a youngling teacher like Tahari. Matter of fact, Tahari introduced us! They're friends from the youngling training camp."

"Well, well! This is the first I've heard of it! When do I get to meet her?"

"After I get done with this assignment. I'm starting a new task, working the supply runs for the tech laboratory in Bataga, bringing the raw wailu kile ore up from the southern mines. I get to see a lot of country from the sky, but that's about it. My next assignment is closer to the city, and I hope we can get together then. Maz should be back, right? Last full moon of summer is my final run. How about it? Celebrate your name day a couple of weeks early?"

"That sounds perfect, Draqkar! Mazkawa should be ready

to come back from training with Cree by that time. We'll have a family reunion!"

"Pa, every time you use my full name I think I'm in trouble!" Maz said, laughing.

"Habit, son. I never shorten student names at the Maga Vihar. At this age I'm not likely to change."

"You're not so old, Pa! Not even five dozens!"

"Maz, I passed that mark four years ago. Cree is only older than I am by two years!"

"Uncle Cree is that old? How is he still working on the farm?

"He does much more than that, son. You'll see tomorrow afternoon. I'll send a pataga at sunrise letting him know we're coming. Birds are cheap to send, so an old Senhan like me can afford it. It's so fortunate that these birds can be so easily trained to carry messages. I think they're easier to train than students, and the process is much faster. It's only a few hours by carriage, if I rent a fast team of horses. We'll leave at first hour".

"Can't we get Draq to fly us out on his new Sikka?" Maz said with a sarcastic grin.

Draq replied, "It's not mine, and you know they can't be used for personal reasons, Maz. I don't get to touch the controls, either. That's only for Ryzen. I'm just ballast, along for the ride unless they need to smelt some ore or examine some rocks."

They all laughed and headed for the door.

"Why so early, Pa?" asked Maz as they walked out of the dinner house onto the cobblestone street.

"I want to get back in time for some stargazing. I'm taking measurements of this oddity's position every night, and I don't want to miss it tomorrow."

"That makes sense. Well, good night, Pa," said Draq, clasping forearms with his father and then his brother. "Good night, Maz. See you in a few months." He headed up the road to the vimana crew barracks, and Maz and Tamu returned to the Maga Vihar residential district, where the family's home was located. Since Maz was done with his studies, he was also out of the student dormitory, and his belongings had already been transferred to his parents' place. Now he would pack up the essentials for an early morning start followed by a three month stay in Banua Zalagi.

Early the next morning, Tamu and Maz headed north on the main road. The horses were as fast as the stable owner promised, and they made good time. Maz was glad he had taken his father's suggestion and worn short trousers under his tunic, as the weather soon became cooler. Instead of the hot, humid climate of the Kamea region, they were entering a brisk, temperate area perfect for growing the crops the area was famous for producing.

Not just crops in the field, either. Maz recognized vineyards, orchards, and forest areas. Every now and then he glimpsed animals in the distance; he knew there were varieties of horned animals like the aurochs he had eaten the night before. Huge boars roamed the forests, so big it took teams of ten hunters to bring them down. It was a good thing they weren't close enough to catch sight of the boars—the animals were fierce, and might attack their carriage.

He knew that even further north the herds of bison grazed, and wild horses—too valuable and intelligent for eating, but a treasured resource for transportation—ran free in the distant mountains. Beyond that, in the north, there were other beasts like the huge mammoth, and other creatures he'd read about in his studies but never seen in real life. The sun was bright, but the mountain breezes kept the area near the Zalagi mountain range comfortable throughout the summer. Banua Zalagi was a huge region that ranged from the edge of the coastal strip to the base of the mountains, and was home to many small townships as well as isolated farming and ranching holds.

The sun was two hours past its peak when they reached Cree's farm. It was a huge holding, with fruit orchards as well as fields of grains and vegetables. Livestock, in the form of varieties of sheep and goats, bleated from hillside pastures and pens. Special enclosures housed chickens, allowing them to roam safely over a limited area. Tamu had described it to him as they traveled, but seeing it in person was different. It all seemed bigger than he'd imagined.

They reached the main house, where Cree's family welcomed them. His daughters, Yani and Wela, rode up to the house on horseback, returning from checking the pastures. Mahani,

Cree's wife, had apparently been baking at the outdoor ovens; Maz hoped that meant there would be fresh bread. Then there was Cree himself, tall and broad, his head shaved in defiance of fashion. Obviously, he followed the Ryzen maxim of not doing anything unnecessary. Taking the time to style his hair, as most men did, was unnecessary, in his opinion.

Like Maz and his father, Cree and his family had coppery skin with a bit of extra brown from the sun. They all wore trousers, woven from cloth, and loose shirts with sleeves to the elbow. The women also wore sleeveless vests that might have been leather, fringed and decorated with beads. Their hairdos were more elaborate than Maz was used to, very different from the women's styles Maz had seen in the city. They evidently didn't follow their father's ideas about fashion, since those hairstyles probably took hours to create, with elaborate braids woven into intricate patterns. The sisters seemed to find Maz's bare legs amusing, making him wonder if he would be expected to wear long trousers while he was here.

Apparently, he would.

"I'll be happy to find you something to cover those skinny legs, cousin," said Yani. Maz could tell the two sisters apart because Yani had at least a dozen blue beads woven into the braids that formed a sort of crown on her head.

"I'll help! No one needs to see that!" Wela laughed uproariously, her topknot shaped into something that looked like a heart, covered with a net of gold beads.

Maz was tempted to fire back with a remark about weird hairdos, but thought better of it. He was here to learn, and maybe the weird hairdos were part of it. He just grinned and let them laugh.

They all went into the house, where a simple meal was ready. Tamu ate quickly and then started his return journey to the city, promising to send a pataga bird with a report of his safe arrival. Mahani showed Maz to his sleeping chamber, which was larger than his cubicle in the dormitory. He thanked her and prepared for sleep, unrolling the bedding as he was used to doing. He washed himself and settled in the blankets, falling asleep almost instantly.

Chapter 3

"Difficulties strengthen the mind as labor strengthens the body. Discipline in all things is the only path to the Ryzen way."

~CreeVa Kau, War Chief of the Nine Tribes, Senior Commander of the Ryzen

It was still dark when Maz felt the covers pulled off him to the strident sound of a horn. He sat up, stunned. What was going on? Without warning, some cloth hit him in the face and his uncle's laugh rang out.

"Up and at 'em, boy! It's sunup in less than two hours! Goats need milking, sheep have to go to pasture! Get your behind moving and get dressed. Your auntie has hot kafi to wake you up. Hurry!" Uncle Cree stood at his feet grinning at him, an aurochs horn in his hand. He sounded it again, laughed at Maz's expression, and left the room.

Maz stood up, realizing the cloth he had clutched in his hand was a pair of long trousers made of heavy, coarse cloth. He hurried into his undershorts, slipped into the trousers (they fit!) and rummaged in his bag for a short half-tunic that he thought would work as a shirt. Those girls would laugh at him if he wore a knee-length tunic over these trousers! He ran his fingers through his hair, tied it at the back of his neck, found the bowl and water pitcher, and quickly cleaned his face and teeth. Feeling almost awake, he staggered out to the kitchen, following the smell of kafi and the glow of firelight and lamps.

His aunt wordlessly handed him a deep bowl of fragrant kafi, sweetened with honey the way he liked it. He thanked her, ignoring his cousins' giggles, clutched it in both hands, and sipped it gratefully as his mind shook off the clouds of sleep.

The whole family was in the kitchen, drinking kafi and talking. Yani's mate was there, too, ready to set to work on his own tasks around the ranch. Their two children, whose names Maz couldn't remember, were eating some kind of porridge at a small table, and Maz suspected their grandmother would be schooling them during the day during her rounds of checking on the livestock and tending to the accounts. Apparently, Maz was supposed to follow his uncle around today, learning about farm life by doing chores.

"Then we'll grab a bite of breakfast after sunup and start your training," his uncle announced cheerfully. "No time to waste if we're going to make a Ryzen out of you before fall."

How could anyone be so cheerful this early? And what sane person gets up before the sun comes up? Maz shook his head and refilled his bowl from the pot of kafi simmering on the hob, added a generous spoonful of honey, and drank it down as quickly as the heat would allow. He set the bowl in the washing sink and turned to face his uncle.

"Ready, boy? Let's get to it!"

The first place they stopped was the goat pen. Cree showed Maz how to milk the goats, taking the right amount of milk to leave enough for the baby goats. They also checked the feed and water troughs to make sure they were filled. Maz had no idea it was so difficult to obtain milk! They went to the cows next, milking those too. The larger animals were a little intimidating, but Cree explained to Maz how to work with them safely. The higher price they got for cow's milk made it well worth the effort.

The milk was packed in glazed clay bottles, labeled with cloth strips, and the containers placed carefully in the cart. Then Cree and Maz hitched a horse to the cart and drove to a large building on the main road. Cree explained that all the farms in the area brought their milk here. The people in charge of this facility sold the milk to vendors in the city and to cheese makers. The money earned was distributed to the farmers according to the amount of milk they brought. Of course, the distributors got their share too. Every farm was an independent business.

Maz found this peculiar. In the city, most people worked for an employer. He was surprised that Cree didn't own the farms and hire workers. It would have increased his profit.

"Then I would trade my freedom for a few strips of cloth! As an independent farmer, I know my family earned every scrap. I helped all these farmers get established, and they paid me a bit at first, but when they no longer needed me I was free of them. I could help them out of love, not greed. It's not bad to be paid in money for help, but it's very bad if you only help for the money.

"Money can be like a chain that binds you. I prefer bonds of love, affection, or compassion. Even duty, which can be cold, is better than greed. I earned the money I was paid at the beginning, but once we had this system in place, I was glad to be free. These people are my friends, not my employees. I traded chains for friendship. I think I got a good deal, boy. A very good deal."

As they continued, Maz learned more about the principle of helping others to be successful. Meat, fruits, grain, and vegetables were sold the same way. Livestock was sold farm to farm, not through a distribution center, but other goods used the same system. Maz learned that Cree had chosen people who enjoyed calculating and record keeping to run these centers, and anyone in the region could apply. The most important requirement was a love of calculating. If the young man or woman didn't love numbers, the job would not be offered.

"You must love what you do, boy, and you must also do what you love. If you love what a Ryzen does, that is what you must do. If serving your realm with your entire body, soul, and spirit is what sets you on fire, clearly you must do that... as I do."

"Do? But didn't you stop being a Ryzen?"

"Of course not! Haven't you been listening? I left the defense forces because I saw an impoverished, starving region with people whose only asset was land. Rich land, but they had no idea how to get it to produce to its full potential. All I did was show them how to do that. In return I got land and a business of my own. Do you see why I was happy to stop getting paid for my help?

"Now I'm a farmer like any other. I serve the realm by making this region prosperous, by representing these farmers as Craftmaster, and by raising wonderful children! I also train the youth of the region in defensive arts, because no peace is guaranteed. I have taught many dozens of dozens of dozens to protect themselves, their families, and their region. I am still a Ryzen. I always will be. I serve where the Creator needs me to serve. That's all."

At midday, they stopped for a brief rest. Cree got some small baked loaves out of his carry bag and they ate them with goat cheese and fresh water. The loaves were made from grains, dried fruit, and nuts—all Zalagi products, of course. Cree told Maz which families grew which products. It was interesting to know, and it gave Maz a new perspective.

"It's almost as if the food tastes different now that I know where it comes from," said Maz. "This cheese came from our family goats. This chunk I'm eating might be from the cranky nanny goat who tried to kick me. Tastes great," he added, with a smile.

"Everything has an origin, my boy," said Cree. "Nothing comes from nothing. It's part of the Way."

"The Way? What's that?"

"It's what being a Ryzen is all about. Our lives align with the Way. It's a pattern made by the Creator that permeates all of life; it's in the smallest parts of our bodies, the tiny, invisible parts that the healers call cells."

"If they're invisible, how do we know they exist?"

"Did you study the human body in that Vihar of yours?" Maz nodded, and Cree continued.

"You learned about the deep-seeing glass, then. The healers look through it and it makes things much larger. The strongest of these are not for young students, but the Senhans of healing use them, and they have seen cells. Our bodies are made up of many-many of these, dozens of dozens of dozens, more than I can calculate. The greatest thinkers among the Ryzen say that the Way is inscribed on these small parts, but we lack the ability to read them. We know the Way exists because we exist, and we know we exist because we are able to think and ask the question. It is confusing to you now, but over the years it will become clearer."

"The Way is in all things. The more you learn of it, and practice it, and make it the essence of your life, the more you will see it in everything. I see it in the hills, the mountains, the stars; I see it in a baby's laugh, in a goat's bleat, in a mammoth's trumpeting cry. I recognize it in every human being I meet. It is life, and more. It is existence. Nothing exists without it, and without it there is nothing that has been made. Perhaps someday we will know the Way more fully, but for now we walk in it and learn from the journey."

"Does everyone know this? What about my father? My sister? My brother?"

"Boy, everyone has the knowledge of the Way, but not all choose to know it and walk it. Your father loves his study of the stars, and doesn't see the Way closer to the ground. I love my brother, but his focus is narrow, and that's also part of the Way. There is a role for the focused as well as for those who see broadly. Your sister sees all things as an opportunity to teach, to inform both young and old, to help them learn. Your mother is a healer, and that's her path. This is how she walks the Way. Your brother is a Vatiga Rishi in his heart, and discovering how to make things and work things is his passion. He is forever taking things apart and putting them back together. He makes knives and tools, because that's a part of his love of making.

"You see more broadly. You always have. This is why you have the potential to be a Ryzen. I saw this in you when you were small. Now we see if you will prove me right.

"We're almost done with the chores. The last task is to walk the fences of the pasture to make sure there are no breaks that would allow a curious animal to escape and wander off. Here, if you follow this fence, you will wind up back at the main barn, the one I pointed out to you earlier. That's where all the families that were hunting in the last bison hunt will gather. One of the animals was kept back for a feast, and it will be at sunset.

One bison will be plenty for a dozen farms and two villages. Those animals are huge!... and very tasty, too! Are you getting hungry?"

"Not really, sir."

"You will be. There's a lot of fence. You will run along the fence and learn to observe on the run. I know exactly how many breaks are in the fence. You will describe them to me when you reach the barn, in about two hours."

"Two hours?" Maz almost shouted.

"Unless you're a faster runner than I think you are, boy."

"Uncle, I have a question."

"Spit it out, boy."

"Why do you keep calling me 'boy'? I have a name."

"Yes, you do, and I might use it... when you're ready. Now... RUN, boy!"

And Maz ran.

He ran for what turned out to be just a bit under two hours, taking careful note of the five breaches in the fence, stopping to repair them and then running again. Finally, Maz reached the barn and ran over to where Cree and his family were gathered, hungry for the delicious meal of the fresh bison smoking and sizzling over the fire pit.

"I'm so hungry! When do we eat?"

"When it is ready, boy," Cree responded in a patient tone with a slight smile." You have to fight for your meal tonight," he added, laughing.

Maz was puzzled. "What are you talking about?"

"It's a tradition here after a successful hunt to have a few grappling contests before our meal," said Cree.

"Contests?" Maz was even more confused. "Yes, grappling, ground fighting". Cree looked at him with a smirk. "Not to death. Just to submission."

Maz smiled back, nodding in understanding. He had been training for over a season now at the academy. He thought he should have an easy time with these village boys. After all, he was Vihar trained!

A nice grassy area had been cleared, and people were beginning to form a circle around it.

"You ready, boy?" Cree asked.

Maz nodded back as he began to prepare himself. He warmed up his joints with exercises he'd learned in training.

"Good, because you are going first." Cree called out to another boy, motioning him over.

"Maz, Dom, greet your partner," Cree said, and the boys touched fists in response.

The boy was about a hand taller than Maz and a bit thinner. Maz looked him over and decided he had this match well in hand. They stood across from each other inside the ring of people. Cree raised up his hand as he paused to look to each boy; then he brought it down with a thunderous "FIGHT!"

Maz closed the distance to his opponent and lowered his body like he had been taught before shooting in to wrap up the legs and tackle his opponent to the ground. But as he dove for the boy's legs, Dom pushed his hips forward and sprawled his legs back, resting his weight on Maz's shoulder. He quickly spun around to Maz's back and pulled him backward as he wrapped his legs around his body and slipped his arm under Maz's chin.

Maz knew he was in a bad position, so he pulled at the boy's arm with both hands, using all his strength to get that arm off his neck. Just as he did that, Dom slipped his other arm even deeper around Maz's neck and locked it to his now freed arm; he slid that hand behind Maz's head and began to squeeze. Maz tried to fight it but it was no use. He began getting a light-headed feeling as things went dark.

Cree was kneeling over Maz as he returned to consciousness. "Good morning," he said with a smile.

Maz looked around to see everyone surrounding him. He was a little embarrassed, but he got up and gave his opponent a hug and pat on the back.

"Thanks for the lesson," he said.

"Thank you for the match," said Dom.

As Maz walked back over to Cree, his eyes were looking straight at the ground. Without looking up, he began to apologize to his uncle for embarrassing the family, but Cree stopped him.

"Boy, you have nothing to be ashamed of. Dom is one of my best students. He's been training five times longer than you. There was never a chance you would beat him; in fact, I'm surprised you lasted as long as you did."

Maz looked up at his uncle.

"Then why did you make me fight him instead of someone that..."

"Someone what?" Cree responded. "Someone that you could beat? What would you learn from that? We learn from challenges and defeats, not victories. Victories only affirm what we have already learned; they teach us nothing. We learn from our failures. We are honored by our victories. I gave you an opportunity to learn, which is much more valuable." Cree motioned back to the circle.

"Come watch the other fights and see what else you can learn, and then we will eat".

Chapter 4

"The true science of the fighting arts lies in practicing them in such a way that they will be useful at any time, and to teach them in such a way that they will be useful in all things."

~ Tome of the Ryzen

The next morning, Maz began his new routine. Every day began with chores, followed by strength training, then training with the weapons. After the morning activities they would stop for a brief meal, followed by running and a swim in the lake. Every day ended with grappling class, where Maz gradually improved to the point where he occasionally won a match. His favorite part of the day, by far, was training with the staff.

The powered staff, the Ichak, was a basic Ryzen weapon, and Maz was looking forward to training with it. However, Cree insisted on working with an unpowered staff first. He gave Maz a staff just a bit below his own height, made of heavy purple wood. It was a good staff, even if it didn't have wailu kile embedded in the tips.

For the first few days, Maz learned basic techniques. His right side was dominant, so his training reflected that. Strong side strike—downward from right to left. Weak side strike—circling around with a left to right strike and bringing the staff to rest under his right arm. Blocks were a daily drill: high block, with the staff raised high horizontally; vertical block, with the staff perpendicular to the ground; low descending block, similar to a strike; overhead block, raised high at an angle over his head, body turned at an angle. Maz worked through the techniques over and over, until they were almost a part of him.

More drills of a different kind took place during his running time. He didn't run alone; Cree ran alongside, teaching him history and philosophy as they ran. Cree believed in the power of memory and repetition, so while they made the rounds of the fences, he taught important precepts which Maz had to remember on the spot and repeat word for word. When he made an error, the passage under study was repeated.

"Hard times make strong men. When times are hard and the people face war, drought, famine, disease, or any natural catastrophe, men and women take up the challenge and become stronger than they have ever been. They become stronger than they ever imagined. Hard times make strong men.

"Strong men make good times. Their faithful and diligent struggles bear fruit. Through struggle the enemy is defeated; through faithfulness drought and famine are made as nothing; through diligence there is survival through catastrophe. When strong men and women prevail, times are good. There is prosperity, peace, health, and safety. Strong men make good times.

"Good times make weak men. When little is required for comfort, some men and women do not struggle. They become thoughtless and lazy. They do not preserve, they do not take care, they do not nourish. The barns are not filled. The watchtowers are dark, the streets are foul, the walls are down. Ease and comfort rule the day. Good times make weak men.

"Weak men make hard times. The enemy creeps past the watchtowers, sickness rises from the filth in the streets, hunger follows the empty barns. There is danger in the skies and in the streets. The fields are unplowed. The mountains crack and floodwaters overpower the land. Weak men make hard times."

Maz repeated the Tale of the Times over and over. He had read it as a child, of course, as was common. He had never understood it or committed it to memory. Now, as he ran along the fences, the words were ingrained in him until he could never forget.

Cree then had a question for him.

"What times are we in now, boy?

"Good times, Uncle."

"How do you know that?"

"We have been at peace for thirty years. There is food to eat, the barns are filled. I've seen them with my own eyes. The forests are full of game. The people are healthy. These are good times."

"Correct, boy. Now tell me, what is happening to the people? Are they becoming strong or weak?"

"The Tale says they are becoming weak, but I haven't seen it."

"No? Reflect on this, and then tell me what you think."

Time and time again, Cree asked him this question, and time and time again Maz had no answer when they reached the barn and prepared for the afternoon's grappling matches.

After a particularly successful day, Maz went up to his uncle, sweat dripping off him like a spring rain.

"Uncle, I think I did well today."

"Not bad, boy. Not bad at all."

"Do you think they'll let me into the Ryzen in the fall?"

Cree looked at him, with the look that usually indicated disappointment.

"Boy, there are two kinds of people in the world. There are some who would ask, 'Who is going to let me?', and there are those who ask, 'Who is going to stop me?' I don't know a Ryzen who would ask the first question."

And Cree walked away, heading for the group going to dinner. Maz stood still for a moment. He sensed that he had just heard something very, very important. It was as if ideas were opening up in his mind, and he realized Cree was right. He had been looking at things from the wrong perspective. He ran and caught up with his uncle.

"Uncle," he said, "I made a decision. I decided I will be a Ryzen, and no one will stop me."

"That's good, boy. When you can come to me and say, 'I am a Ryzen,' instead of 'I will be a Ryzen,' you will have reached understanding."

The days passed, until nearly a month had gone by. Maz learned more than he ever had at the Vihar. He was learning philosophy, history, human behavior, farming, care of animals, cleaning, cooking, and how to sew up a rip in his trousers. He could build a fire and cook a meal of what he had gathered or hunted. He could build a shelter from a sudden storm. And, of course, he could fight, with staff and blade and body.

He was also learning to think. Much to his surprise, he discovered he was not really accustomed to thinking. He could read and discuss other people's ideas and opinions, but his own opinion was usually based on the opinions of people he liked. Gradually, he was learning to form an opinion based on his observations and on solid information.

One day, towards the end of his first month of training, Cree asked him again if the times were making weak men. Maz had been thinking about it, and he had his answer ready.

"The times are good, Uncle, and I see a few things that might be signs of weakness. Back in the city, there are people who will not work. They say there is no respectable work for them, that they are philosophers who observe the human condition. They demand to be paid a wage for this, but are not willing to write about their observations or give lectures at the Maga Vihar in exchange for a wage. They say every person is entitled to food and shelter and healing simply by being alive.

"They go to falu pau or inns and demand they be fed and offered a bed for the night. No matter that they could have a bed and food if they worked for an employer or committed to study at the Maga Vihar; they go to the businesses of people who are working for a living, and demand what they sell, but won't pay for it. They ask healers to tend to them, but offer nothing in exchange. Their claim is that everything should be given as freely as sunshine is given. What concerns me is that innkeepers and healers are listening to them. They feed these 'sunshine people,' as they call themselves, and then brag about it on street corners, as if they had done something great.

"I didn't see before that this is a sign of weakness. The ones who demand have become weak, but so have the innkeepers and healers who value their work so little and aren't strong enough to stand up for themselves.

"I also see what caused my father concern, so that he brought me here so you could teach me. I took my exams at Vihar. When I was given the opportunity to correct my errors and have a perfect result, I refused. I said it was good enough.

"That is where it starts, Uncle. Settling for what is good enough, doing less. It is not so long a step from doing less to doing nothing. I don't have the whole picture, but I do see this small part of it.

"Good. Keep thinking. Keep looking. Now, here's another thing to think about."

"The Way has no hindrance. Nothing can stop it, nothing can prevent it from succeeding. Why is this true?"

"I don't know, Uncle. Not yet. I will know soon, and I'll tell you."

"Good. You're right. You don't know this yet, but you'll know it soon. Now, here's another question.

"A wise man once said: 'There is nothing outside of yourself that can ever enable you to get better, stronger, richer, quicker, or smarter. Everything is within. Everything exists. Seek nothing outside of yourself.' If this is true, and the Way is also true, it seems to be a contradiction. But both are true. Explain."

"I can't explain it today, Uncle. I'll explain it soon."

"Good. Now pick up the pace and see if you can beat me back to the barn. You have matches waiting."

The lessons continued. Maz began to see everything in a different way. He no longer accepted what people told him; he used it as a starting place for investigation. Even Cree's pronouncements were starting points for further consideration. This was a new thing for Maz. He had never questioned what people told him; he accepted it all, no matter how illogical. Now, however, he found himself questioning everything, testing to see if it was true. Once something was proven, however, he didn't continue to question. He began to distinguish between proven and not proven, and it seemed this was exactly what Cree wanted him to do.

This pattern followed into his physical training. In grappling, in staff training, and in blade work, Maz learned to spot tricks and traps. He also learned to set traps for his opponents, leading him to win a greater portion of his matches. Even when he was sparring with the staff, he learned to spot when his opponent was leading him and could avoid falling into a trap.

Staff training fascinated him. He was still working with the wooden staff, because Cree wanted him to have mastery of the wooden weapon before he trained with the metal wailu kile-infused staff, the Ichak. This traditional weapon came from ancient times, and the making of it was a secret lost in the past. Modern Rishiken could repair minor problems and maintain the energy, but if an Ichak was completely destroyed it could not be replaced. Only the Ryzen were permitted to train with them. If he made it into the ranks of the Ryzen, he would be issued his own weapon. Until then, he used a wooden staff constructed to be the same weight and balance as the real thing.

The Ichak could be used in every way a wooden staff could be used, but it had additional attributes. Energy emitters were embedded in each end of the staff, to send out incredibly strong force rays. The rays could repel, attract, or destroy by manipulating gravity the same way Sikka do. Cree had demonstrated this with his own weapon, blasting apart a rock with the destructive energy, disarming an opponent by pulling a weapon out of his hands with the attraction energy, throwing an opponent many cubits away with the repellent energy.

"You must be so familiar with the staff that no mental effort is used to move it precisely where you want with exactly the power you want," Cree said. "You must be able to focus your mind on the energy of the weapon, not on what you're doing with the staff itself. That must be nearly unconscious; we say it must be "without mind", Mu shin in the old language. No need to think about a strike, a jab, or a block; just do it, freeing your mind for other tasks. Mu shin is the state you want to achieve for anything. This is very different from having no thought because you are lazy or ignorant! This transcends thought. Your knowledge must be so deep that conscious thought isn't necessary. That's what we're working towards."

Cree practiced many other disciplines, as well. There was one he did every morning after rising. Maz had seen him do it a few times. It was called the Art of Poses, and it involved standing or sitting in a particular pose for a certain length of time, then shifting to another pose. The poses had names; Hungry Bear, Sleeping Mammoth, Falcon on the Beach, and so on. There was one called Vimana Rising. Maz thought it looked easy and asked if he could try it.

"You think you can do this? Do you want to learn the Art?"

"No, thank you, Uncle, not yet. I'm sure I'll need it when I'm old, to help me stay in shape. But I just want to try that one pose. It looks easy."

Cree shook his head. "I thought I'd run that out of you, boy."

"Run what out of me, Uncle?"

"A liking for what's easy. Well, then, you can work this easy pose. Do what I do."

Maz tried, and tried, and tried. Over and over, and he couldn't get it. After what felt like a dozen dozen attempts, he fell flat on his face and couldn't get up without help.

"Well, boy? Was that easy?"

"No, Sir! It looked like an old man's easy exercise, but I just can't get it!"

"Well, I tell you, boy, it might be you're just not old enough yet."

Maz realized he'd been led into a trap again. He was better at spotting his uncle's tricks, but he still fell for too many of them.

He needed to improve if he was going to get into the Ryzen in the fall!

One afternoon, near the end of summer, when Maz had been training with Cree almost three months, Cree paused for a moment near the end of their run to compliment Maz on his improvement in grappling.

"You're not bad, boy," Cree said. "You win more than you lose, and you've won your last ten matches. I normally train each student twice a week, rotating groups, as you know. Three groups, each twice a week. If we gave achievement vests for grappling the way the Ryzen do for overall growth, you'd be almost a blue vest. That usually happens after a year of intense training. I've worked you three times as hard as anyone, even including when I trained new Ryzen."

"Thank you, Uncle."

"Don't thank me, boy! I'm doing this for a reason. We need strong men to counteract all the weak ones. Something's building, not just here but with our friends to the east. I think they may not be as friendly as we think. I may be training you for battle. Real battle, not mock battle. Not just sparring."

Maz was stunned. "You think there might be a real war? But... I just had a letter from Draq. He's in the defense forces, and he didn't even hint at anything like that."

"What did he say?"

"Just that he was looking forward to finishing up this assignment. He's running a pickup and delivery schedule from the wailu kile mines to the observatory, the manufacturing sites, and the Maga Vihar laboratory. I guess it's a bit boring, just going over the same route over and over. He has a lady he's in love with, and their schedules don't match. He hasn't seen her in weeks. Most of his letter was about how her beautiful dark curls float in the breeze," Maz said, in a high pitched voice, waving his hands like a breeze. "It's kind of funny."

Cree looked at him, puzzled. "Your brother is on a delivery run with the most valuable substance in the world, running the same schedule over and over, so everyone knows where they'll be and when they'll be there?"

"I guess... wait a minute. Did you just say what I think you said?"

"That your brother is unwittingly setting up the perfect conditions for a robbery by greedy thieves, or even worse—a raid by enemy agents? You heard me, boy. This could be trouble. I think when I take you home in a couple of weeks, I'll drop in and have a word with the Sages, just a hint, and then bring your brother back here. I think tomorrow we'll add knife fighting to our training program. Now, let's get on with it. You have battles to win."

Training intensified in the last two weeks remaining. They spent less time on farm chores than on running, fight training, the new knife fighting sessions, and memorization. Once while they were running, Maz asked Cree if there were books he could read instead of rote memorization.

"Yes, all this knowledge is in books. But answer me this: Do you want to read it or learn it?"

"Learn it, of course, Uncle!"

"Reading will give you knowledge about these things and where you can find the information later when you want to access it. Learning is different. Now tell me this: If you were going into a fight, would you rather read about staff fighting or train it?"

"Train it, of course, Uncle! I see what you mean. Memorizing something, saying it, explaining it—these things put learning inside me. Things I learned from books—you're right, I have an overview of them and I know where to look them up when I need more."

"Exactly. I'm all in favor of books, boy. They have their place. The things I'm teaching you while we run are things you need inside you without any time lag. Some things can wait, like the date of the Council of Nochi-Lan or the names of the Nine Grandmothers. You can take a minute to look them up. Learning how to research, how to look things up, is valuable. But when it's really important, when lives are at stake, the knowledge must be embedded in body, mind, and spirit. These are the things we learn as we run."

They ran in silence for a while. After a summer season of daily running, their skin was a deeper copper color than at the start of the season, since they ran with their shirts off and tied around their waists, because of the heat. His long, dark hair was in topknots on top of his head, keeping it off his back and neck. Cree's shaven head was starting to make sense to Maz. Their trousers were usually sweat-soaked by the end of a run, but going without would have been unwise, since they ran through brambles and tall grasses that grew along the dry lakebed that was the usual route. Maz had never been fat, but after three months of intensive exercise he realized he had been carrying some fat around the waist; that was gone, and he had added muscle on his legs, arms, and chest. His stamina had increased, though his uncle still surpassed him in both strength and endurance.

"Boy," Cree said, "I'm going to teach you something that just might be the most important thing yet. You're going to begin learning the Code of the Ryzen. I'll give you the whole thing, and then we'll break it down in pieces. Ready?"

"Yes, sir!"

Cree recited the Code from memory:

"I proudly serve as a guardian of my fellow man, always ready to defend those who cannot defend themselves. I do not seek recognition or adoration for my actions. I voluntarily accept the danger of my calling, placing the welfare and security of others before my own. I serve with honor on and off the battlefield. The ability to control my emotions and actions sets me apart from other men. Discipline in all things is demanded. My training is never complete. I am always learning and always humble, without ego. I will constantly train my mind, my body and my spirit to be stronger than my enemy. I train to fight and I fight to win. I will uphold the proud tradition, the ancient teachings and the legacy of those that have gone before me. I stand ready to fight. My action will be swift and violent but guided by the principles I am sworn to uphold. Uncompromising integrity is expected. my character and honor are steadfast. My word is my bond. I will never quit."

Chapter 5

"Though we may try to hide the truth, it cannot long be concealed."

~ Prophecy of the Nine Grandmothers

"System checks complete. Ready?" the Ryzen captain asked the ship's passengers, both trained mineral specialists, Vatiga Rishi who were assigned to the Sikka Manu.

"Yes, sir." Draq, the junior team member, was still new at his new post on the three-man ship, so he wanted to make sure he did everything correctly.

"Strapped in and ready, sir. We're good." The other Vatiga Rishi, Hiku Nau by name, was a little more relaxed. The team worked well together on their routine supply runs, bringing messages and essentials to the miners and evaluating and transporting the latest load of precious ores.

The seed shaped Sikka lifted straight up into the air and hovered for a moment as the Ryzen pilot laid in the course. Kal Kama was an experienced pilot, the sole Ryzen on board and flight leader, with hundreds of flights logged to his name. His Ichak staff glowed in its holder, powering the ship and responding to the pilot's mental commands relayed through his dark gray Ryzen helmet, the color of tempered metal inlaid with strands of glowing wailu kile, the mineral that powered their ancient technology. His thoughts, focused through this ancient headgear called "capaicha," which translated to something like mind-link in the ancient tongue, were backed up by his hands on the controls. The Sikka Manu were truly wonderful machines, and Kal was an excellent team leader. Draq knew he was lucky to be assigned to his ship, the Charging Mammoth, named for its unusually large crew chief, it's size and cargo capacity also matched. It could carry more of the precious wailu kile ore than any other Sikka in the fleet.

The Mammoth lifted silently off the ground, straight up until it cleared the tops of the trees that surrounded the airfield. Kal manipulated the controls, visualizing his intent, and the seed-shaped craft stopped its ascent, held position for a moment, and sped off to the right towards the shore. The airfield was northeast of their destination, a mine located near the coast at the congruence of ley lines where the immeasurably valuable veins of wailu kile were located. Their team was tasked with harvesting the substance and bringing it back to the Maga Vihar laboratory, as well as the main laboratory in the Citadel, where it would be carefully placed in power capsules. These would then be distributed to those authorized to receive the carefully guarded source of power for weapons, healing treatments, and many other uses, not the least of which were the Sikka Manu airships that protected the people of Timur Laut.

Draq Kau, who as the junior Vatiga Rishi was trained in the science of metals, ores, and minerals, scanned the control panel as they shed power in flight and regained it when Kal flew the craft over ley lines. The flight pattern was designed to take advantage of the power the wailu kile cells absorbed as they flew over the invisible lines that crossed the earth. Just as a healer could work with the energy lines to promote healing and recharge the cells in the body, the ley lines recharged the cells of the Sikka Manu.

Draq Kau had worked hard to qualify as a crew member. He had not qualified for the Ryzen, the elite order that protected the nation and preserved the ancient knowledge. He hoped Maz would honor the family by qualifying for that elite group, and if anything could prepare him for the test, a summer with Uncle Cree was just the thing. Nevertheless, though not a Ryzen, he served the Makarishi, the Nine Ancient Ladies who ruled the nation, as one of the Vimana that formed the most honored part of their national defense forces. As a minerals expert and trained Vatiga Rishi he had won a much-coveted spot on one of the magnificent silver flying craft.

The Sikka Manu was the not-quite-secret shining star of the vimana force. Large enough to hold a crew of three plus a decent amount of cargo, the sleek ovoid discs traveled at unheard-of speeds, moving through the air more than ten times as fast as a man could imagine; countless times faster, even, than the swiftest predator bird in a swift dive. They flew as high as the heavens, but could hover close to the ground if there was the need to do so. No other people on earth had such marvelous aircraft, and very few in Timur Laut were privileged to see them, much less touch them. In fact, the average person considered them magic.

Many of the Vimana flyers were one-person craft, the sort found throughout the nations of Timur Laut, from the great continent to the western islands. The small craft were mostly used for urgent communications too sensitive to trust to a courier on foot or on horseback, and too lengthy for trained courier patagas. The small flyers were limited, so the Sikka Manu, the magnificent large airships, made up the heart of the nations' defenses. A craft that was big enough to carry precious cargo and a crew practically guaranteed that no country would ever again take up arms against Timur Laut. The peace secured by the Great Treaty of thirty years ago would hold forever, that was certain.

The "flying rooms", as the Sikka Manu were sometimes called by villagers outside of Timur Laut, had been reclaimed just in time to turn the tide of the Great War. They were artifacts of ancient times that the defense forces hadn't used in centuries. With the urgency of the Great War, the Ryzen called upon their greatest minds, the Sages, who figured out how to get them in the air and operate their weapons systems. The huge flyers were armed with energy pipes, similar to the tubes some tribes used to blow darts at the enemy in close combat, but much more powerful. Their "darts" were pure force, like the energy that propelled the aircraft, but the energy capsule that activated them was powered by a single grain of the rare wailu kile, producing a beam of deadly, devastating force. The craft was also supplied with more deadly weapons, the Ryzen themselves wielding Ichak, the double-tipped energy staff for which the Ryzen were famed. Swift, powerful, and well-armed, the Ryzen fleet with its Sikka Manus made their nation almost invincible. Draq Kau was immensely thankful to the first people that the high knowledge existed, that the Sages, the greatest of their scholars, had reactivated it, and that he was privileged to ride in the almost-magical craft.

#   #   #   #   #

Outside the Wailu Kile mine, South Coast

"Shh! Careful! You're making more noise than a herd of goats!"

"Yes, Senator Brakos," his captain whispered. He hid in the brush, trying not to flinch when the plant's thorns stabbed him.

"This mission is more important than your comfort, or even your life! You know what this means to us!" The tall blond haired Senator managed to convey menace in a near-silent hiss.

"Yes, Senator Brakos."

"Everybody else get the message? We go in quietly."

The other four shadowed figures in the brush murmured "Yes, Sir" in subdued voices. Their names were Stercos, Degos, Kanos, and Dynasis, and they had no intention of arguing with him. They were all a bit afraid of Brakos' temper. He was huge, nearly five pixos in height, five times the length of a man's forearm. His mass and strength matched his height; his enemies claimed his father was part Yigantes, and he didn't correct them. It pleased him that the common men thought he was descended from the legendary giants of old. He didn't think it was true; his father was tall, certainly, but no giant. Any giantish ancestor had to be centuries back. Nevertheless, the story kept his subordinates in a state of fear, which was a good thing. He valued the members of his personal guard, but it was better if they remembered who was in charge.

"Now, listen carefully. We need to take out the Ryzen first. He'll be wearing a vest of some kind, probably blue, or maybe gray with blue piping and feathers. I don't think they'd send a higher rank on a routine mining pickup. Even so, he's dangerous; he's likely to be the only one trained to fight. He could take all of us all by himself, if he is able to use his staff, so we have to surprise him. If he has a thing on his head, we need to get it off. That's how they control their weapons. The others should be easy to deal with. There will be two more with him; because this is a mine there will have to be a specialist in ores, or maybe two of them, if they're still doing things the way they did when I was at their training vihar. The others aren't trained to fight. Get the Ryzen, and it will be like spearing fish in a barrel." His team nodded in agreement.

Forty pixos in front of them, just outside the mouth of the cave they'd been watching, the dirt flared up briefly. A Sikka Manu descended and stopped in front of the cave. Three men got out and went to the cave, moving quietly. Brakos and his minions waited in silence, and after about an hour the crew returned, with the Ryzen pilot in the lead, carrying a large leaded casket. It was clearly heavy, since he needed both arms to lift it and wasn't carrying his staff, which would make it easier for Brakos.

The area around the mine was only lit by the flickering lights of the torches mounted on the outside of the mine entrance. The crew were not far in, but the sun was going down and provided little more than a faint glow. Kal, who was not wearing his helmet, carried the casket containing the wailu kile to the side of the Sikka; suddenly he stopped and looked back towards the entrance, listening.

"Did you hear something?" asked Draq, stopping just outside the mine entrance. Ita was right behind him.

"We need to get moving," answered Kal. "Let's pack up and get out now. Something's not right."

This was only Draq's first mission, but even if it was his twelve dozenth he would never question a Ryzen. Without another word, they quickly finished loading the rest of the ore, precious metals almost as valuable as the wailu kile, and their mining tools into their carry bags. The gear included a metal box specially designed to carry the waliu kile so nobody would get sick from it; it was well known that prolonged contact with untreated wailu kile caused a wasting sickness that required long treatments to recover. Some people were so sensitive to it that even brief contact to their skin made them break out in blisters. As they walked out the entrance the sun was sinking over the horizon. Kal motioned them to stop; he listened briefly, then silently set the box down on the ground. Without warning, a spear pierced his chest; a second one followed, and Kal fell to the ground with a grunt. Draq and Hiku stood frozen in shock. Brakos emerged from the shadow of the trees and confidently strode up to the two remaining men, followed by his team.

"Thank you for the gifts. I assure you, they are much appreciated," he said as he moved in closer.

"What are you doing? We are not at war, and you just killed a Ryzen!" Draq was outraged, still not understanding what was happening. He pulled a knife out of its scabbard; the one he had crafted it himself out of rare metals in a beautiful layered pattern, and had placed his maker's mark on the blade where it met the hilt. Now, he wondered if he might have to use it.

"They will hunt you down!" He gripped the knife.

"Oh I'm counting on it," said Brakos, "and there's more. You're not going to like this next part." He grinned and took a step towards him.

Draq raised the knife high, blade pointed down, and aimed an overhand strike at the pirate; Brakos quickly overpowered and disarmed him with a swift grip to the wrist, twisting his hand back towards his chest and taking the knife from him. Then, without warning, he plunged the knife into Draq's throat. Simultaneously, Kanos and Saltos of his crew took care of Hiku with their own knives, one blade through the back and one blade in the neck. Brakos looked down at the blade in his hand, it was made of a metal he'd never seen, unbelievably sharp, curved with a wide middle and narrow point and perfectly balanced. It was a work of art. Such knives were rare. He calmly wiped it on Draq's sleeve, took the scabbard and replaced the knife in it, placing it on his own belt. "Nice knife," he said.

"Hide the bodies!" he ordered. Stercos and the others hurried to obey. They dragged the silent, unmoving crew into the bushes, hiding them under the dagger-like fronds of the bushes, brushing tracks away with branches. It wouldn't delay discovery very long, but every hour gained was more time to mobilize the Theralonian forces. Less than half the armies (soldiers and sailors) were willing to listen to him, but Brakos knew that once he landed the flying ship on the Nesos training grounds and his team carried out the casket of magic ore, these half-convinced soldiers and sailors would be entirely on his side. A few more covert attacks on airfields, a few more flying ships captured, and he would have them following him into battle. Then it would be easy to convince the rest of the Senate and the Assembly to vote with him. With the recent death of the King, and his son too young to rule, at the age of only ten years and a few months, the Senate held all the power in Theralonia for the next few years. It was truly a fortunate time for him to be a new Senator. If his plan worked, Timur Laut would be his before the winter solstice. With such a victory, then those senile old Senators would all listen to him, they would bow before him–and so would the vast isle of Theralona. Everyone would want him as Basilos, the elected king, instead of that little brat king now sitting on the throne, because with such an accomplishment, what else could he be but the true king?

Brakos' men were excited. An easy battle, a treasure beyond belief! They didn't mind sailing their ship without their leader; he had commandeered the Sikka and, using the knowledge he gained years ago when he studied at the Maga Vihar in Timur Laut, lifted it off the ground. The crew walked back to the beach and boarded their high-prowed ploios. This ship could travel the seas, yet had a shallow enough keel to pull up on the beach. Between the sails and the oars, and a strong wind, they would be back in Theralonia before three sunsets had passed.

While they sailed, Brakos flew the Sikka just over the waves. He had only learned the basic emergency controls for the ship, since he had not continued with his training, but it was enough to begin with. He planned to figure out how to fly it effectively. There was another vein of the magic ore on the north coast of Timur Laut, and a pickup was scheduled for the day after the next full moon, a mere ten days away. He would fly with a team, and since he couldn't fly more than one at a time he would have to capture a pilot, steal another flyer, get more magic ore, continue until he was ready for a big strike, and godhood would be in his grasp.

The winds were with them, and they reached home long before the third sunset. The crowds on the dock flocked to see the amazing flying ship as Brakos landed it on the pier;

he disembarked, and the sailors carefully loaded it on a huge cart and wheeled it to a warehouse along the shore. Opening the huge doors of the warehouse on Brakos' orders, the sailors maneuvered the craft into the sheltered space that normally held new ships and ship building materials. Brakos' family owned the warehouse, part of their ship building company, and business had been slow of late—which was why Brakos planned to store captured flying ships in the family's empty buildings. Their fortunes would be restored soon enough, when his plans came to fruition. War was good for business when you are the only ship builder on an island nation.

As he had expected, a crowd gathered. Brakos was good with crowds. He began with an impassioned plea to the Assembly to call for a vote on the question of going to war against Timur Laut.

These despicable wizards, he insisted, were plotting to conquer Theralona, and might succeed unless their beautiful island kingdom defended itself. He brought out the casket of wailu kile, and the glow when he opened it was so bright the people looked away. Brakos touched his little finger to the shining ore, and was pleased to see he hadn't been mistaken. The one time he had encountered the ore, his skin broke out in a rash immediately. Brakos didn't know if everyone would react that way or if he was sensitive to the substance, but it worked. The skin of his finger immediately became red, with tiny bumps popping up on the surface. He sealed the box again and showed everyone his finger.

"Poison!" he said. "Foul poison! The wizards want to poison our people with this vile substance, else why did we find it in a flying machine? They plan to drop it on our cities from the air!"

The dockside crowds were largely ignorant, uneducated people who were likely to believe anything. Brakos was counting on their gullibility; he was a very charismatic politician, but facts and truths were not helpful to his plan. A few more successful raids to stir up the Ancient Ladies of Timur Laut, more persuasion applied to the sailors and soldiers of Theralona, and the plan would come together perfectly.

Back at his ship, Brakos called the members of his personal guard together. Stercos, his voice hoarse as usual, was the most enthusiastic.

"Sir! What's next? Are we going to go get another flying ship?"

"Precisely. All of you-make preparations, have your weapons ready. Bring ropes to tie up a pilot or two, we'll show everyone what real warriors can do! I promise, within a month you will all be officers in my new army the Assembly and Senate will persuade the King to authorize. Mark my words! We sail with the tide."

Chapter 6

"Death is certain for the living, and life is certain for the dead; therefore, you should not grieve for what is inevitable."

~ Tome of the Ryzen

Back in the citadel very early that morning, before the sun rose, Tamu took his gaze from the far seer in the observation tower. He blinked and rubbed his eyes; they were sore from looking at the stars all night. Thankfully, he had no lectures today and would be able to get some much-needed sleep. The anomaly was still there, and it was clearly getting closer. He was trying to measure its progress in order to estimate its speed and trajectory. It was proving to be a more difficult task than he had anticipated.

He put his paperwork away and prepared to leave the tower. As he approached the stairway, he heard voices from the level below.

"I need to see Senhan Tamu Kau immediately. This is urgent business."

"I don't know what to do, sir. You wear the Ryzen uniform, sir, and I respect that, but the Senhan told me not to disturb him in his tower, not for anything! Please understand, I'm new here. I don't want to lose this position. I have to do my year of service, or I won't get into the graduate program next year!" Tamu's administrative assistant, Kimo, sounded upset; Tamu hurried down the stairs to see what was going on.

There were two Ryzen standing there; a man wearing a flyer's uniform with the blue feathers of an experienced Ryzen, probably a Crew Chief, and a much older woman with the brown hood that indicated a high ranking Ryzen. The hood was trimmed with brown fur, not made entirely of bear fur as the hood of a Senior Ryzen would be, nor did she have the bear claw trim on the necklace and belt worn by those who were closest to the Sages. Her dark hair was sprinkled with grey, worn in two braids. A seasoned instructor, then, with years of service.

"What's going on here? What do the Ryzen want with me?" He peered at them through sore eyes and had a better look at the Crew Chief, seeing a moderately young man, perhaps just under three dozen years old, tall and slender, his dark hair in a braid down his back, with the yellow fringe cords of a Hokulani wayfinder dangling from the hem of his vest, along with the traditional blue feathered scapular.

"I'm sorry, Senhan. I wouldn't disturb you if it were not a serious matter." The Blue spoke, a well-trained, respectful voice, showing the courtesy that marked the Ryzen.

"A problem in navigating by the stars, friend?" The man smiled; evidently he knew by the prominent yellow glyph on Tamu's red tunic that Tamu was a member of the Surida Ka, a religious sect that believed all people should be in friendship with each other. Any Surida Kai would address anyone as a friend, and most of them treated others as friends, too.

"I'm glad you call me friend, sir. Where may we speak privately? I am here with the senior Ryzen known as Petra, and she has an official message for you. I am Lupo, at your service; when we are finished I will take you wherever you wish to go. I have a Sikka waiting, sir."

"You sound very serious. Speak freely right here, friend. I have no secrets from Kimo, and I'm too old to be going up and down stairs. And please no need to be so formal, call me Senhan, or if you do not wish to, call me friend. Now what has brought you here?"

"As you say, sir… I mean, friend." Lupo bowed politely, the shallow bow that indicated respect from one human to another, but not the deep bow that would be given a superior. Tamu appreciated that; people of his beliefs did not give or receive deep bows except to the Creator. Tamu sat on the stairs, and gestured for both of the Ryzen to do the same. They preferred to stand, and Tamu began to be concerned at the serious look in the Ryzen's eyes.

"Senhan," said Petra, stepping forward, "it is my sad duty to inform you that Vatiga Rishi Draqkar Kau has lost his life while in the performance of his duties as a member of the defense forces in service to the Grandmothers and the people. Is there anything we of the Ryzen can do for you?"

Tamu stared blankly, disbelieving. He could hardly believe it; Draq dead? "Bahi! Have you told his mother? Cree. I have to go see my brother, Cree. And my son is with him. I have to get Mazkawa and take him to his mother, she will need her other son there for strength."

Petra nodded. "We have not contacted your wife yet. I will personally see to it. We will send two Sikka Manu with you, to carry your family members back to the citadel. I will bring the news to Bahi and bring her back to Tambak Citadel. Lupo has a message for senior Ryzen CreeVa Kau, so he will accompany you. Is that satisfactory?"

Tamu nodded, still stunned.

#   #   #   #   #

Maz caught up to Cree just as they reached the barn. He was smiling. Maz presented his staff to his uncle in the traditional manner, on his two open palms held a cubit apart. Cree bowed and reached for his weapon, and then stopped, frowning.

Maz heard it, too; the low hum of a Sikka. He looked around and saw not one, but two Sikka Manu flying in. Cree waved his arms in the traditional "safe to land" signal, and the two vehicles set down a little way south of the barn. Each vehicle held two people, and one got out of each. Maz recognized one of them as his father, running shakily towards him, stumbling. The other, a man in the Ryzen uniform with a grey vest trimmed in blue, caught Tamu as he was falling and helped him walk to Maz. He looked familiar to Maz, who wondered if this was the Ryzen from the testing center. The older man clutched his son and held him close; Maz held him tightly and realized he was sobbing.

"Pa! What happened?"

His father said nothing; he just kept on sobbing, holding on to Maz as if he intended to hold on to him forever.

The Ryzen stepped up to Cree and bowed. "Sir," he said. "Friend."

Cree returned the bow. "I see you, friend. Tell me."

"I am Ryzen Lupo Kai," he said, "crew chief of the Sikka 'Darkwolf'. In service of the defense force and the Nine Grandmothers, I bring a sealed packet for senior Ryzen CreeVa Kau."

"I'm Cree. Let's have it."

"Here, sir."

He handed Cree the packet. Cree opened it and read what it contained. He took a deep breath, turned to look with understanding at his brother, sobbing in his younger son's arms, and looked back at the Crew Chief.

"Did you find him?"

Lupo didn't pretend to misunderstand.

"I did, Do you want the full report now?"

"This packet told me enough for now. You can tell me on the flight back to the citadel. I'll ride with you so Maz and Tamu can ride together. What of his mother and sister?"

"I believe both will meet us at the Maga Vihar. A flyer was sent for each."

Cree shook his head. "This is bad. Very bad. It may go deeper than we think."

"I agree, sir.

Cree went over and detached his brother from Maz, hugging him fiercely.

"I know, brother. Weep as you need to weep." He reached out and included Maz in the embrace.

When Tamu's sobs subsided, Cree handed him a cloth to wipe his face. It was sweaty, but Tamu didn't notice.

"He's gone, Cree. My boy Draq is gone. They found him under a bramble bush. My boy is gone."

#   #   #   #   #

The short flight back had taken only a few minutes to find the landing pad on the cliffs of the Citadel. Maz and Cree returned with their bags. Cree had activated his emergency orders, leaving leadership of the tribe to his wife Mahani, who was also a senior Ryzen in her own right. Her specialty was healing, like Tamu's wife Bahi, but she could train fighters quite well. After thirty years, she and her husband knew each other's jobs as well as their own. With his home and district in good hands, knowing his daughters would back up their mother, Cree was able to turn his attention to Lupo's story.

"I went looking for them, Sir. They were two days late returning with the wailu kile. The Grandmothers were concerned; they had a "knowing" that something was wrong, and they called for the nearest Ryzen. They spoke, and I went."

The Nine Grandmothers, whose ancient name was Makarishi, were the supreme rulers of the entire Northwestern continent. Cree nodded. If they spoke, you went. It was that simple.

"I went on a short ship to leave room to bring someone back quickly," Lupo said. A short ship ran with two Ryzen pilots, It was a common practice when there was a possibility of needing to transport wounded, to make more room in the small craft.

"We reached the site, but there was no one there. The landing and takeoff signs were there to read, so we knew the Sikka had arrived and gone. At first we saw no sign of the crew, but then I noticed there were no footprints. If they had landed, loaded, and departed, there would have been footprints in the moist soil. It looked as if marks had been brushed away with branches. The two of us continued to search, and we found three bodies hidden in the bushes. We brought them back to the citadel, where I received these orders. I think those are the most important points."

"And what did you learn of the atack, chief?"

"It looked like a quick death, sir. No signs of torture. By the signs, they were ambushed and killed quickly. The Ryzen, Kal Kama, had two spear wounds in his chest, one through the heart. The other two, including your nephew, had their throats cleanly slit. There would have been no long suffering."

"That's good," Cree said. "A warrior's death, That boy would have been scared enough without adding more suffering. What else, chief?"

"They took the wailu kile and the Sikka Manu, Sir. It wasn't a random quarrel. This was purposeful."

"I feared this would happen." He paused. "Do you know the rest, chief? Were you told what my orders are?"

"I was, sir. senior Ryzen Petra informed me before we spoke to your brother. We are presumed to be heading for war, and the Grandmothers need a War Chief. They wish to open the Pyramid of the Elements and call the Ryzen to lead the war."

"We are already at war." Cree said solemnly.

#   #   #   #   #

Back in Tambak Citadel, Cree saw his sister Bahi waiting for them to arrive on the landing pad and a wave of sadness passed over him. She was a strong woman, but nothing can prepare one for the loss of a child. Draq was his nephew, and he still remembered the pain of losing men in battle, but this was… her child. Hopefully he would never know that level of pain. As soon as they set down and the door opened, Bahi rushed to them and threw her arms around Tamu. They held each other for a long moment, eyes watering, sobbing. Maz joined and all three hugged as tight as they could. Cree went over to do his best to briefly comfort them. "I promise you, sister, this cowardly act will not go unpunished. Unfortunately, I must leave now; there is official business I must attend to, but I will meet up with you soon".

Lupo waited patiently, feeling a mix of awkwardness and uselessness for witnessing so much of what should be their private grief, powerless to do anything to ease their pain. In time they were ready, and the elder Ryzen who had gone to get Bahi now took Tamu and Bahi to see Draq's body and make arrangements for his funeral. Maz waited behind in the open receiving area, because Tahari was due to arrive soon. She hadn't yet been told of their brother's death. Lupo remained with him, answering his questions about the Ryzen. Since Lupo admitted he was the Ryzen from the testing center, Maz was full of questions—anything to avoid talking about Draq. Filled with compassion, Lupo answered him instead of deflecting his questions, but he still insisted on calling him "mouse." Maz started by asking about the Ryzen vests.

"You start as a new vest, mouse. The vest is a light bone color, since it's made of unbleached plant fibers, but we call it simply a new vest. My vest is made of the same fibers, trimmed with a bright blue braid down the front and around the arms, as you can see. The dye comes from a mollusk of some kind and is the same color as the blue feathers we wear for formal occasions, which is made from the discarded feathers of the northern thunderbird. That's all I know. Clothing isn't an area of study for me. I wear the uniform on duty, and off duty I wear what I buy from clothing vendors.

"I've been training for eight years. In fact, I could be your training supervisor if you pass the test, since I'm due to take a new trainee after one of my crew is promoted. I'd be working with you until you wear the blue feathers, and then you would train with a higher rank. Your whole life is training. There isn't training time and not-training time; you might be off duty, but a Ryzen is always training. Even the Sages train, though they train alone sometimes.

"I don't know if I'll ever be assigned to train with Senior War Chief Cree, but I hope so. That's up to the... who in the stars is that?" Lupo asked, as he stared at the woman who had just walked into the room. Her long dark curls flowed halfway down her back, held off her face by a coral band. She was dressed in a hokulani's uniform, but instead of a Ryzen vest she wore the knee length belted overtunic of an unmarried woman, in a deep coral shade with a woven yellow fringe.

"Maz!" she called out, as she walked quickly towards them. "Where's Pa? What's happened? I got a message to come to the main hall's reception area. That's all I know. Is something wrong with Pa? Where's Draq?" She spoke quickly in a low, pleasant voice. Lupo stared at her, clearly stunned.

Maz grasped her hands. "Maybe you should sit down, Tahari." He led her to a bench in a corner. Lupo followed, still silent.

"It's Pa, isn't it? He's not... he's not gone? Is it his heart?" Her eyes filled with tears.

"No, Pa's fine. It's not him. It's..." Maz couldn't speak.

Lupo stepped forward, facing her, as he noticed how lovely her eyes were.

"Tahari Kau, it is my solemn duty to tell you that your brother, Vatiga Rishi Draqkar Kau, has given his life for his people. He is with your ancestors. I'm very sorry for your loss. Please tell me how I may be of service to you."

She stared at him as if he had been speaking Nesish.

"What do you mean? Draq is gone? That's not possible! He's three years younger than I am! He's barely an adult! He can't... he can't..."

"He was murdered. I'm so sorry to have to tell you this."

"But why? Everyone liked him! He had no enemies!"

"His team was ambushed at the wailu kile mine. The bandits stole the entire crop of Wailu Kile as well as the Sikka Manu. They were killed quickly; their throats were cut. It doesn't appear that they suffered long. It would have been quick."

She stared at him, trying to understand what he was saying; Lupo saw in her eyes when the meaning sunk in, and she broke into sobs. She turned to Maz, weeping on his chest. He patted her on the back, trying to comfort her. Lupo stood by helplessly, wishing he could do something to ease Tahari's grief.

Soon, she was able to stop weeping. Lupo handed her a cloth to dry her face; he seemed well-supplied with kerchiefs. The next hours, as they waited for Tamu, were filled with tears and long silences, broken by reminisces of Draq as a child. This was pain beyond anything either of them had yet been forced to bear.

#   #   #   #   #

The best of the drum slowly grew faster, filling the room. Smoke from the herb-scented bonfire drifted on the faintly stirring breeze that blew through the open windows cut at intervals in the clay walls of the ceremonial clan house. Every member of the Kau tribe was entitled to wear the tribal symbol and use the clan house for funerals, naming, and all the ceremonies that marked passages of life.

A high, lilting melody joined the drum; the pipe seemed to speak to something deep within the soul. After a while, a voice added its notes in harmony. Sounds at first, then words, as Cree stepped forward to bid farewell to his nephew. Tamu should have sung the farewell, but he couldn't speak of Dra without tears, so he asked Cree to sing for him. He did, in the nasal chant that recalled the ancestors and traditions of house and clan.

If Draq had been Ryzen, the ceremony would have been different; a mountain instead of a house, a dance instead of a song. But Draq was not Ryzen, so his farewell was one of family. The song began.

I come today

Today

Today

To sing the Creator

And of one

Who walked among us

Called by the Creator

Shaped by the Creator

Guided by the Creator

Who walked among us

As a baby

As a child

As a man

Who found his name

Son

Brother

City dweller

Who found work

Flyer

Fixer

Vatiga Rishi

Who walked

Who danced

Who laughed

But he is gone

And we sing loss

We sing grief

We sing mourning

Then, the song became a wordless chant as each person around the fire shared a memory of Dra. There were childhood memories from friends and relatives, memories of the Maga Vihar, of flyer training, of the peculiar antics of Vatiga Rishi, of flying high above the earth. Some told of jokes played on friends; some told of challenges met, of races won. A young woman shared hopes that now would never be fulfilled.

Tahari stepped forward and told of her memory of a younger brother following her around the house. "I stopped him from falling into the cooking fire. I could not save him from the enemy's knife."

Bahi, Draq's mother, spoke through her tears of him bringing her little toys he had made. "I was so proud of him. I am proud of him today. I will be proud of him tomorrow, and all the days yet to come."

Maz spoke of a much loved older brother. "I wanted to follow him everywhere. I cannot follow him today. But I will see his enemies ground to dust."

Then Maz took over the chant while Cree spoke. "This nephew was dear to me. I will not forget him. I will walk the path where his death leads me. I will fly, I will climb, I will fight, and I will slay."

Tamu stepped forward. He struggled to speak; Bahi came up behind him and put her hands on his shoulders. Drawing strength from her touch, he opened his mouth.

"I had two sons. Now one is gone. There is a hole in my heart."

The people stood in silence for a moment. The casket bearing Dra's body was lifted on two horizontal poles. They reminded Maz of fighting staffs, and his resolve to take the fight to the enemy grew stronger. Maz, Cree, Tahari, and three flyers from Draq's cohort lifted up the poles. The rest of the mourners took up the chant, and they followed the casket as Draq was carried by those who loved him to the funeral pyre in the courtyard, where he would rejoin with the earth and sky to rest with those who made the journey before him. The fire ceremony was done in complete silence.

#   #   #   #   #

The next few days were busy ones. Lupo, along with his crew of two other Ryzen, Sidu Ma and VasDef Lau, and another Sikka with a crew of three, consisting of two Ryzen and one non-Ryzen Hokulani, had all traveled south to the mine where the ambush happened. Their mission was to set up a lion-watch, as a lion would do waiting for prey. This had to be done without being seen, to find out who, if any, came back to the site for more Waliu kile.

They parked the Sikka Manu a thousand pixos back from the site and hiked in quietly to get a visual. Once they established that nothing was in the area, they brought the Sikka closer, covered them, and set up a hidden base camp. The Hokulani, Chimma Tak, remained with the Sikka while the others rotated shifts between three overlook positions, staying hidden in the foliage.

The first two nights were uneventful. They watched, ate food, drank water, took care of personal hygiene. On the third afternoon, Lupo was on watch when he and the rest of the team spotted a ship coming from the east. It was circling the mine and their position, obviously looking for something. Lupo's team remained hidden. The craft approached, and they could see it was a Sikka. Lupo recognized it as the stolen one; it was painted with new colors and markings, but Lupo knew it was the same.

Unexpectedly, two more Sikka Manu arrived from the same direction and circled above in the same pattern. The first craft landed, and the others followed. They watched a tall man dressed in purple-trimmed white robes, wearing a laurel wreath on his head, get out of the first Sikka with two others. Lupo knew the man instantly; he was Brakos, a former Maga Vihar student who was exiled for misconduct. All three men in the first Sikka headed into the mine.

Lupo wanted with every fiber of his being to attack this arrogant infiltrator. However, it would be dangerous to move on Brakos now, since they were outnumbered three to one. Their mission was to gather information, not fight a battle. They would stick to the plan, remain hidden, and bring the news back to the War Chief CreeVa Kau.

They waited patiently as Brakos and his crew came out with a heavy metal box, loaded up into the ship, and prepared to take off. Clearly, the regular mine staff had continued their digging schedule, leaving the raw ore in the normal place for the Sikka teams from the capital to pick up. If they were in the area, the miners would assume these Sikka Manu were the ones who ran the regular pickups. Lupo was thankful that the miners had gone to the next mine, or no doubt they would have been killed as the others had been. The Sikka lifted off, forming up in the circle pattern above as the crew from another Sikka loaded and took off. The process repeated with the third ship.

When all three were loaded, they rose up in formation, and flew off at a surprisingly low altitude. They did not rotate back with belly forward in the typical Sikka fashion for long speed and distance, but simply maintained their orientation and headed off toward the east. It was as if the pilots were still learning to fly; this matched what Lupo knew of Brakos' experience with the Sikka Manu, that he only knew the level that was taught in basic flying classes. He had, presumably, taught a couple of others of his own people, by the way all three Sikka Manu were flying; low altitude, slow speed. Emergency flying methods, which were taught to students so they could use a Sikka Manu in a disaster, to escape and get help. This was good news; the raiders had not managed to turn a trained flyer to their cause. It was just Brakos and his henchmen, and they were soon out of sight.

Lupo's team loaded up and headed back to the capital to report to the Makarishi. No doubt, they would cancel further mining until the situation was handled. Recognizing Brakos had been a stroke of luck, or an act of providence by the Creator; a much younger or older team would not remember an obscure exchange student from Theralona. This bit of information told Lupo that the mine robberies and killings had, in fact, been the work of an enemy of the nation and not merely the actions of a thief. Brakos had been a wild young man, greedy for fame and fortune; he was certainly no different now that he was older. His purple trimmed tunic was proof of that. Only members of their government were allowed to wear purple, so he had probably been elected to that office. Senator, maybe. The laurel wreath was worn by ship's captains, and it was further evidence that Brakos was in a position of power. Now, he probably wanted revenge on the people who expelled him for misbehavior. The Grandmothers would definitely need to know about this. Soon after they reported back to the capital citadel, the Ryzen induction ceremonies were scheduled, and Lupo wanted to attend. He would be Maz's training Blue, assuming he passed his entrance test, and besides, Maz's sister would probably attend the ceremonies. He had no intention of missing any opportunity to spend time in her company.

Chapter 7

"There is more than one path to the top of the mountain."

~ CreeVa Kau, War Chief of the Nine Tribes, Senior Commander of the Ryzen

The Ryzen entrance examination covered three areas; body, mind, and spirit. The applicants being tested were gathered at the Ryzen training camp outside Tambak Citadel, sipping cups of kafi while they waited to be called. Maz was surprised to see a familiar face; Dom, the young man who beat him in his first grappling match in Cree's barn. Cree had been training him, too. He caught his eye and nodded in greeting; Dom nodded back, with a smile. There would be two of Cree's students testing today, it seemed.

The examination began with the tests of the body. First was a foot race on a short track; both Dom and Maz finished well, keeping pace with the Blue who ran with them as the standard marker. The test focused on who could match or beat the standard, not who could beat other applicants. It was different from competitive foot races, and Maz realized that, for the Ryzen, competition was with yourself more than with others. Could you meet the standard and continue to better yourself?

That was more important than whether you ran faster than any other person testing. It was a different point of view for Maz. He suspected it wouldn't be the first time that the Ryzen Way was different from the way he was used to. At the end of this race, all went on to the swimming and climbing challenges, but only those who kept up with the standard marker would continue on to the rest of the examination. All of these received one blue feather from the nest of a thunderbird. As a new vest, they would continue to accumulate these feathers, which would be made into the blue feathered scapulars they would wear with their formal uniform when they were promoted to the rank of Blue Feather, the instructor's rank, usually just called Blue and represented by blue braid on the shoulders of their everyday vest.

Next came the swimming and climbing challenge; a large, man-made lake on the training grounds was the venue. The applicants had to swim around the lake a dozen times before swimming to where a wooden platform floated at anchor. They had to touch the platform, take a brightly colored cloth flag, and return with it to the dock where they began. Though it was a simple test,it wasn't easy, and Maz struggled to keep up with the Ryzen mentor setting the pace. He was tired to the marrow of his bones when he reached the dock, wet flag in hand. Almost there; one more challenge to go until he earned the feather for the combined event.

Then came the climbing part of the test. Maz was not so sure about this one, as tired and wet as he was.. A bar was set up across the top of two poles, about twenty pixos in height. The challenge was to climb up a thick rope attached to the bar, grab a flag from the top of the bar, and climb back down without falling. This was more of a challenge for Maz than the previous two tests, and required the most effort. Climbing had not been a major part of his training up to that time. More than once he slipped and lost ground, having to climb back up and continue. He was tempted to take it easy, since he had succeeded at the other two challenges, when he saw Dom standing nearby waiting for his turn. . Maz couldn't let him do better in this test! He saw Dom watching him,, and he climbed almost up to the top, tried to grab the flag, and slipped back down about three pixos. He was exhausted. He adjusted his grip, gained a pixos in height, and slipped again, down five pixos. Twice more he tried and slipped before reaching the top. The last time, he slipped all the way to the bottom, landing on his backside on the ground.

Discouraged, all he could think of was his test back at the beginning, the day he failed. Do your best, Lupo had said. Do your best. Did his best include giving up? He realized it did not, and he rubbed dirt on his hands and tried again, determined to succeed. This time he got halfway up before he slipped, but he managed to stop before he reached the bottom.

Why wasn't this working? He had done this kind of climb before. He had never failed at any physical challenge. He couldn't fail today. It was simply not possible. He hitched himself back up, using his feet and legs as well as his arms, creeping up one finger length at a time. He lost track of the minutes as he climbed; his muscles were on fire, and he couldn't think, just move one hand at a time, one foot at a time, over and over. It seemed he had been doing this for hours, days, even weeks, when finally he was less than an arm's length away he attempted to twist his arm around the rope for a better grip so he could reach out for the flag. It didn't work; his arm gave way and he fell to the bottom, landing awkwardly on his ankle and twisting it painfully.

Refusing to give up, he dragged himself to the base of the rope and started to reach for it when the mentor for this challenge stopped him.

"That's enough," he said.

Maz looked up at him. "No, I will do this!" He staggered to his feet and stumbled as he tried to put weight on the twisted ankle. He grabbed at the rope, missed, then caught hold of it.

"I said that's enough," said the Ryzen. "Here is your flag." He handed Maz a worn, dusty flag in a different color from the one on the bar.

"Go and take this to the table," he said.

Maz took the dirty flag and fought to hold back tears. He had failed. It was almost more than he could stand. Determined not to show what he was feeling, he limped over to the table and handed the worn flag to the senior Ryzen standing there.

"Here is my flag, sir," he said.

Much to his surprise, the Ryzen smiled. He took the flag from Maz and handed him a blue feather.

"No one passes the rope, boy," he said. "The feather goes to those who don't quit until we tell them to stop".

Maz turned around to see another candidate fall from the rope. The young man was clearly upset, and he stormed off, mumbling about impossible tasks. Finally, Dom had his turn. Like Maz, he fell repeatedly, but kept going, and didn't stop until he was told to do so. He, too, got a worn and dusty flag, which he exchanged for a feather.

Maz realized this challenge was not about climbing a rope. It was a test of determination, to see if a tired candidate would keep trying until there was no more to give, when a Ryzen told him he could stop and get his hard earned worn, dusty flag; this was what it took to be a Ryzen. It took determination and a refusal to quit. This, ultimately, was his reward; the knowledge that he would not quit.

That evening's test, the mind test, was a simulated night mission, in which the candidates had to enter a heavily-guarded tower, remain undetected, and surprise the Ryzen Blue instructor at the top, securing a flag from his belt. Maz waited at the tent set up at the base gathering point as the first two returned without flags. This would take some strategy, it seemed.

Maz realized that a direct attack on a defended position was not the best idea, so he had to figure out a different solution.

He had learned that lesson in his talks with Cree. As he walked around, considering the situation, he realized the four-sided tower had two open windows, with one of the non-windowed sides backed up to a tall cliff. When it was his turn, he circled around to the back, taking care to avoid being in a direct line of sight from the windows at the top. Circling around, he scaled the cliff, still out of sight of the guard position, and climbed to a tree on the cliff just below a corner where the irregular stones of the tower provided handholds. Just barely out of the windows' sight, a branch extended a few foot-lengths below. He slowly and stealthily climbed the tree, with his ankle still sore from his earlier fall which he did not want to repeat now. Quietly making his way along the branch to the window, he heard steps as he walked to the opposite window, and quickly hoisted himself up and through the window, came up behind the Ryzen's back and caught him in a choke hold. The Ryzen tapped him on the arm. Maz let go, recognizing the traditional submission. "Well done," said the Ryzen, handing him a bright blue feather. Tucking the feather carefully in his vest pocket, Maz climbed back down the same way he had come.

He returned to the tent, seeing Dom ready to head up to the tower. Sometime later, Dom returned to the tent holding a feather; Maz grinned, glad that his friend had also passed the test. Maz did a quick count and realized that only five were left out of the original dozen applicants. Four had failed the physical tests, and three were eliminated by the mental test. He and Dom would both move on to the last test, a test of spirit. Neither one of them had any idea what that would be like. How do you test a person's spirit? Maz couldn't think of anything. The next part was set for sunrise the next day, so he got a good night's sleep in anticipation.

They all met outside a tent set up at the base of the mountain. It was just before sunrise; Cree had sent another Ryzen to represent him, as his duties as War Chief kept him occupied. Two senior Browns were there, along with a handful of Blues who assisted in training the candidates. The senior instructors explained the last part of the test.

The task given the final candidates was to collect at least one of the rare blue thunderbird feathers from a nest they would find at the top of the mountain and return by sunset. It was not an easy test; it would be a challenge to get from the base to the top and back in a single day, much less search for a thunderbird's nest and extract castoff feathers. If the nest contained eggs, they would have to deal with an angry thunderbird, as well. There were several nests around the summit, and not all would have blue feathers. There was no standard marker for this test. Making it back with at least one feather was the entirety of the test, as long as they made it back before sunset. Maz, Dom, and the three other candidates were allowed to make preparations and bring whatever they thought they might need; food, water, tools, and any other items they could carry that they thought would help them.

They all started up the mountain at the same moment, from different points at the base of the mountain. Although there was a paved path with a wooden railing all the way up to the top, they were not allowed to use the path. Five unpaved trails were marked, each one originating from a different point at the base. They were allowed to find a different way up the mountain, but it was strongly suggested they stick to the marked trails. When Ryzen "suggest" something, it is a good idea to pay attention, thought Maz.

Maz brought a treated leather bag filled with water, some dried meat and fruit, a loaf of flatbread. He also had iron stakes to use in the climb, a small jar of ointment and cloth wrappings for wounds or blisters, a long, thin rope, and a hat made of leaves to protect his head from the sun. He thought he had anticipated every challenge they could give him.

At first, the climb went as he had expected. He carefully rationed his water and food, remembering that he needed to make it last the whole day. He paced himself, hoping to reach the summit by the time the sun was at its highest, and pick some time on the return journey since it would be downhill.

About three hours into the journey, he came upon something unexpected; an old man lying along the side of the trail. His clothing was covered with the dust of the mountainside. He was obviously in pain, and moaned when Maz touched him.

"What happened to you, friend?" Maz said, falling into the way he had been taught to address others.

"Friend? I hope so. I need a friend," whispered the old man. "I wanted to climb to the top of the mountain, because there is a meditation garden there. I started climbing at sunset, planning to greet the sunrise from the garden. It is supposed to be a beautiful sight. I tripped and fell. I think I broke my ankle. Will you help me back down the mountain?"

Maz considered the request. He had a few options. He could simply refuse and go on his way. He could give the old man water, bind up his wounds, and promise to send someone to help him down once he returned to the base, trusting that the old man would somehow survive. He knew there were wild mountain cats here; he had seen tracks and scat. Or he could abandon the quest and bring the old man down himself, hoping he could hurry back up in time to make his target. If his return trip was very smooth, with no difficulties at all, there was a chance. He chose that option, since for Maz there was no way he could leave an old man at risk on the mountain. He realized it would be much more difficult; so be it. It was necessary.

Maz carefully picked up the man and began the return journey. It took longer than he expected, since the journey pained the old man, and they had to stop twice along the way, once for the old man and once for Maz and his own ankle beginning to hurt again. They reached the base just after midday, and Maz took the old man to the area around the tent, where the Ryzen were waiting.

"I found this man on the road," he said. "Will you take care of him while I hurry back to the top?"

"No, candidate," said the Brown Ryzen waiting by the tent. "That's not allowed. We can't leave this area in front of the tent. You'll have to take him to a healer's house, or to his own home. The test is the most important thing."

"Can I just leave him here? I'll take him to the healers when I get back."

"Why don't you ask him if he wants to be left here?"

Maz turned back to the old man, who was sitting in the shade of the tent.

"Friend, I'm in the middle of a test and I must continue. I haven't found anyone to take you to the healers. Will you be willing to wait here for me? I'll give you all my food and water, and I'll probably be back after sunset. I'll take you to a healer when I get back."

"I will be happy to wait," said the old man. "Let me thank you for bringing me back and taking care of me. You show your generous spirit by your actions."

And the old man took three bright blue feathers from his pouch and handed them to Maz.

It took Maz a moment to figure it out. He had passed the test. The Ryzen in the tent began to congratulate him, and asked him to wait in the tent to see what happened with the rest of the candidates. They had food and drinks in the tent, and the old man stood up and congratulated him, walking on perfectly healthy legs into the tent. He introduced himself; he was a Sage of the Ryzen, named ChoGun Miya. He grinned as Maz stared at him, awestruck. How had he not realized the old man's dirty, dusty clothing was all black, including his long vest? He saw only the dust. He would not make that mistake again.

Not much later, Dom returned, also carrying an old man. Maz had the fun of congratulating him, too. Cree had taught them well, it seemed. Of the three remaining, two had left water and food for their "old men", and one had simply apologized and continued his quest. The three returned at sunset, having found no thunderbird feathers at all. There were no nests at the top of the mountain, only a meditation garden and a shrine dedicated to the principles of charity and compassion.

#   #   #   #   #

"The Way, being supreme, has no hindrance."
From the Tome of the Ryzen

There were many dozen people lined up, standing in rows on the sandy floor of the arena. All the candidates wore "no vests", the standard everyday attire consisting of a short tunic and ankle length trousers in a light tan color, the natural shade of the plant fibers they were made of. Maz stood in his place, dressed in his candidate clothes, looking around in amazement. The arena was so much bigger than he imagined!

At one end of the rectangular open structure, a raised podium rose several hands above the ground. On the podium the

Yudansha Rishi, the Sages of the Ryzen, sat in a row, their legs tucked under them. They wore black pleated, wide-leg trousers and woven black sleeveless vests, open over plain sleeveless black tunics. Their arms were covered with tattoos, telling the story of their notable accomplishments. Each one held an Ichak in his or her hands. Dozens of bone-colored vests and blue feathered scapulars rested on low tables in front of the Sages.

A Senior Brown Vest Ryzen stood behind each Sage. The Senior Browns, according to their custom, wore their knee length fur-trimmed vests over waist length, short sleeved white tunics and blue trousers, symbolizing their internalization of the qualities of each rank they had attained. The blue trousers were a reminder of the attainments they reached while learning and serving as instructors; the brown fur trim, from the hide of the short faced brown bear, was a reminder of their success in hunting and in battle. Their short sleeves showed forearms decorated with tattoos. Taking turns, each Senior Brown called out a candidate's name. The candidate bowed, walked to the podium, and bowed again in front of the Senior who called him or her. Then, at a word, the candidates each sat on the ground in front of the Sage. The Sage, using the power of the Ichak, floated a vest over to the candidate, who received it on two open palms, then stood up without the use of hands, bowed to the Sage and Senior, then returned to the ranks. Once back in line, the candidates put on the bone-lined, light tan hip-length vests, trying to be as graceful as possible.

Finally, it was Maz's turn. The Senior Ryzen standing behind an old man, who Maz recognized with pleasure as Yudansha Rishi ChoGun Miya, was his uncle Cree.

"Candidate Mazkawa Kau," he said, and Maz bowed and walked to his uncle, bowed again, and sat in front of the Sage, going down on one knee first and then the other, his hands pressed together in respect.

The Sage smiled at Maz, then lifted his Ichak and gestured. A vest lifted gently off the table and floated towards him, as he placed his hands in front of him, palms up. The vest landed perfectly on his upturned palms. It was much heavier than he expected. He got up, using only his legs, bowed, and returned to his place in line. Once the next person was called, he quietly put on his vest—the vest that made him a Ryzen. It fit perfectly, of course. It was stiff, since it took many months of wear before the fibers of the vest softened. He liked the stiffness, but he knew a softer vest was a sign of experience. He would wear this vest every day until it was too ragged to wear, and it would be ceremonially burned when he acquired a new one.

When all the new vests had been distributed, the distribution of blue feather promotions began. To Maz's surprise, his uncle stepped forward and addressed the crowd. His voice carried throughout the arena, and Maz wasn't sure if this was due to some kind of Vatiga Rishi device or simply Cree's own abilities.

"Now we will acknowledge those of our own who have trained with us along the Way. After a time, those who train reach a greater understanding of what we do and take on more demanding tasks. They are ready to teach, and become instructors. We recognize this with a visual sign, the blue feathered cowl that covers the upper chest, neck, shoulders, and upper back with feathers earned in tests and in service to the Grandmothers. The instructor's everyday uniform will reflect this with a blue braid on the vest. This is an outward sign of what is already a reality. The one who wears the blue feathers, or the blue braid on his vest, is a mentor, a helper of those who are newer on the Way. That is the primary charge on a blue vest; to train and encourage. They have other duties in their job or profession, but this new responsibility is the essence of what the blue feathers mean, and why the instructors are blue vests.

"A blue feather is not mere authority. It is more like the uniform of a guide. If you go climbing in the mountains, you want a guide. You listen to what your guide tells you, not because the guide has authority over you, but because the guide knows how to be safe and how to get home. This is why a new vest listens to a blue; not from fear, but because the person with the blue feathers has more knowledge of the Way."

Cree then began to call names. Following the Blue investiture, the ceremony ended. All the new Ryzen recited together the Code of the Ryzen. Then they dispersed; Maz and his family and friends, including Lupo, headed for the falu pau, looking forward to food, drink, and time to visit and talk about what the future held for all of them.

#   #   #   #   #

It was still dark. Maz was rudely awakened when his bedcovers flew off him, landing on the floor. Lupo stood at the foot of his bed.

"Time to get up, little mouse! The sun will be up in less than an hour!"

Maz groaned.

"Do they teach that? Is it part of the Way? Is the idea of sleeping forbidden in the Ryzen?"

Lupo laughed. "We've all been awakened this way, mouse! You'll do it, too, when it's your turn. I'm happy to follow in Senior Brown Cree's footsteps. Get up!"

"All right, all right," Maz grumbled. "What's so urgent?"

"Your first assignment as a member of the Ryzen, of course!"

"What? I have an assignment? Why didn't you say so? Let's get going!"

He hurried through his morning routine and within a short while was hurrying to keep up with his chief as he strode swiftly across the central courtyard towards the flying field. They reached a three sided shelter in which a Sikka Manu rested. The symbol on the side looked to Maz to mean Running Dog, with the glyphs painted in blood red paint.

"What do you think of the Darkwolf?" Lupo asked him.

"But... but... it says Running Dog," said Maz. " Maz made a scrabbling movement with his hands, like a running dog's paws.. " I think that's a good thing.." He gave Lupo a sly grin to show he was teasing.

Lupo saw the humor, and turned it back on Maz. "They're very similar, little mouse, but when it is enclosed in the diamond form, it's the sign for Darkwolf.. Most people who don't know their history would say Running Dog," he said, giving Maz a sly grin in return. "They would think, as you probably did, that the diamond is just to emphasize it. In fact, when you enclose a symbol like that it takes on its ancient meaning. The flight team and the ground crew call her the Darkwolf. It's the name of every ship I serve as crew chief. You've heard of the legendary Darkwolf?"

"Yes, but that's just legend. Like dragons and flying serpents. They aren't real, either."

"They were real once. It's Ryzen lore, mouse, and it's true. In our spirits, there is a conflict. Some say there is a good wolf and an evil wolf, but My people and the older legends say it is a gentil wolf and a fierce wolf. The gentil wolf is called the Light Wolf, the heart of the pack, who is gentle and kind and is the peacemaker. The fierce, strong wolf, the one that defends and protects the pack, is called the Darkwolf. Both are necessary, and both reside in each person, we choose which spirit to bring out and when, the gentle or the fierce. Do you see? We draw from our legends and make them real. Like this Sikka, for example. She is the protector, and therefore she has the fierce soul of a

Darkwolf. When you get to know her better, you'll understand."

Lupo looked fondly at the sleek craft. Clearly, the flight crew had a good relationship with the machine.

"It's a beautiful Sikka. I'm proud to be part of her crew."

"Good. Now hurry and drink that cup of kafi. You need to finish it before you get in the bird. I don't want kafi spilled on her."

Maz did so, hurriedly gulping the hot beverage and then climbing up the ladder to the cabin on his first Sikka assignment. The cabin was surprisingly roomy, bigger than most and much larger than it looked from the ground. Maz was told to sit in the main pilot seat. When he questioned Lupo about it, the mentor Ryzen laughed.

"Don't go thinking it means you're in charge, mouse. I'm in charge. It's my duty to teach you to become the best pilot I can., and I will tell you where we need to go from the hokulani seat and do the wayfinding; Jebal is the weapons and systems master, and so he's in charge of everything else. For the foreseeable future, your job is to sit in that seat and do what you're told. You're in training, and your job is to learn as much as you can as fast as you can, and all I expect is for you to give it everything you've got, and become the best pilot in the fleet. No pressure. Oh, and use your staff if we run into trouble. Yours is the purple wooden one." He indicated a side panel fitted with brackets holding three staffs. One was the wooden staff Cree had used during practice; Maz recognized the purple wood. Cree had given him his practice staff! The other two were light metal Ichaki, presumably belonging to Jebal and Lupo.

"Got it. Shut up and bash the bad guys."

"You're a quick learner, mouse."

Maz settled in his seat and looked over the mysterious controls, fascinated by the symbols.

"Hey, new one!" called a voice from outside, somewhere in the depths of the shelter. "You're not going anywhere yet!"

Maz looked out the window of the Sikka. He saw an unusually tall, muscled man about Lupo's age in a worn and faded blue-trimmed vest, the everyday field uniform of a Ryzen, carrying a staff. He was spinning it one-handed, grinning.

"Better get out there, mouse," Lupo said. "Looks like you're about to meet another Ryzen tradition!"

"Huh? That guy's a tradition?"

"Not exactly, but what happens next is. Come on, let's get out there!"

Lupo grabbed the wooden staff and handed it to Maz, then took the other two Ichaki and brought them along.

When Maz, Lupo and Jebal descended from the craft, it became obvious that many more had been invited to this "tradition". About two dozen Ryzen were there, mostly wearing blue-trimmed vests, but there were a few with soft, thin new vests, too. All wore either the flyer or the field uniform; these were some of Maz's new co-workers. Apparently this was some kind of rite of passage.

"Good. You're ready." The large Ryzen challenger quickly ran through the opening moves of the classic invitation to spar, a downward and upward block followed by a left vertical block. Without thinking, Maz responded with a right to left strong side strike, and the sparring began.

The Ryzen wasn't as good as Cree, but he was better than any others Maz had sparred. He had a hard time keeping up, narrowly escaping some nasty bruises as he miscalculated the force or direction of a technique. He found himself on the defensive, parrying strikes and jabs, deflecting thrusts, avoiding sweeps at a furious pace. After a hand of minutes he was sweating profusely, breathing heavily as he fought. Finally, he misjudged a block and the opponent trapped his weapon, sending it clattering to the ground. He reached for it, but it was snatched from his grasp.

"Not so fast, new one! If you drop your weapon, you have to do a dozen pushups to get it back. Don't you know anything?"

Maz had no idea if this was a real thing or something made up but without hesitation he dropped and did a dozen pushups, sweat dripping in his eyes. He stood up, wiping the sweat with his hands and then wiping his hands on his pants. He looked around.

"Hey, where's my staff?"

"I reclaimed it," said a familiar voice. "If you're going to be dropping your weapon, you'd better drop your own instead of mine."

Of course, Cree was there. Maz realized he wasn't surprised. He had clearly been set up.

Lupo spoke. "His old weapon seems to be missing, sir. Perhaps he could use this one." He stepped forward and presented an Ichak to Cree, extending it with both hands. Cree took it from him and stepped closer to Maz.

"Good idea. Maybe he'll take better care of this one." He held it out to Maz.

Maz realized this was an elaborate way of giving a new Ryzen his first Ichak. He had never seen this one before; it had clearly been hidden until this moment. It was a dull grey metal with the faint glow from the reinforced metal ends, holding the precious wailu kile mechanism. He bowed and received the weapon on his outstretched hands, taking hold of it with the traditional two-handed grip. It was the most beautiful weapon he'd ever seen; it seemed to glow just for him, gleaming brighter when he touched it, and the staff warmed under his hands.

The entire group burst into cheers. One by one they came up to greet him, slapping him on the back and demanding a sparring match in the near future. His original opponent, who introduced himself as Melikai, complimented him on his technique and wanted a second match at the next training session.

Cree placed a helmet on his head, the traditional capaicha of the Ryzen that would allow him to link with the Ichak and with the Sikka. It was much lighter than it looked; Maz had expected it to be much heavier, but it felt like nothing at all, except for a tingle at the temples. The other Ryzen lined up and, one by one, they smacked him on the top of the head, making the helmet ring. It was evident that they all needed to make sure the helmet fit right.

Maz realized he had not only gained a weapon; he'd gained a troop full of new friends. With every smack on the top of the head, he felt more and more part of the group, more truly a Ryzen. Best of all was his uncle's look of pride.

"Good match, Maz. You did well. No new recruit has lasted more than half a minute with Melikai in years. I guess you learned something over the summer, after all!" His uncle was the last to smack the top of his helmet, and he did it with such intensity that Maz staggered a bit, and grinned at his uncle. It was the best day of his life.

# # # # #

Training, strategy sessions, surveillance flights and more training all began to blend together as Maz's first several weeks as a Ryzen flew past. There were so many new things to learn, it almost dulled his grief about his brother, he had no time to think about anything besides learning his new position in his crew.

New policies were put in place to guard against ambushes, but they still took place, although with less success. Mining parties doubled in size to provide for armed guards at the mine entrances during a harvest. Eventually, a guard patrol was permanently stationed at each location. Coastlines saw patrol boats cruising at every convenient landing place, and this alone prevented enemy ships from hitting the coasts without warning.

One battle that Maz overheard recounted over and over in the falu pau took place off the coast, about a three-hour sail to the south. The village fishers were out in their boats when they were attacked by a Theralonian piloi, a type of ship used by raiders as well as shore defenders. The long, many-oared sailing ship was swift and maneuverable, and the crew were armed with bows. They had standard arrows and fire arrows, and they shot the fire arrows at the fishing boats, trying to catch the sails on fire. Other archers aimed their regular arrows at the fishers themselves, sometimes from very close range. In one case, that proved to be their undoing.

An arrow struck a tall fisherwoman, the boatmistress of one of the larger boats, and she was not happy. Leaving a small girl holding the tiller, she shouted a command and her crew of fishers jumped across the narrow space separating their boat from the piloi. Dark hair flying in the breeze, they were armed with oars, staffs, and long spear-headed staves called nagatini that were usually used to spear large fish. This crew of healthy, active young men and women, accustomed to fighting wind and wave and large fish, gave the Theralonian crew a fight they had never before experienced. Within minutes, they were all tied up with ropes, smarting from hard strikes with the oars and wooden staffs, and the nagatini's sharp ends ripped many a shirt and left the wearers bleeding.

It was reported that the boatmistress laughed and said they should have known better than to come after Timur Laut fishers with only a crew of twenty. An even match was sure to end in the fishers' favor.

"Next time bring a hundred to take on ten of us, and you might have a chance," she reportedly said. Her crew, along with the two small boats in their little fleet, lashed ropes to the piloi and hauled it back to their village, and then transported them overland to the capital. The piloi joined the fisher fleet, after they repainted it and gave it a rude name. It was said to have increased their yield of fish threefold, when it was put in service. Maz loved hearing the stories, and thought how much he would have liked to have been there for that one, and been part of the fight..

The stories came in from many other villagers, too, who did their part. The far-southern port of Yucanitsa served a half dozen villages, who pooled their resources to institute foot patrols at intervals and signal flames to warn the coast. One unfortunate Theralonian raiding ship, unaware of the warning system, landed their shallow-keeled craft only to be ambushed as soon as they stepped on to the sand, with the whole village turning out to fight with farming implements, cooking pots, and grinding stones attached to handles. One small boy was proud of bringing down a huge sailor all by himself, by sneaking up in the dark and smashing his kneecaps with a stone hammer. He was the hero of the village children for many days afterwards.

Maz himself began to have more dangerous assignments as the war heated up and his team became proficient at spotting enemy raiders. He increased his skill with destructive energy, but his focus was still on piloting, learning all the tricks of the Darkwolf and how to maneuver skillfully and "make her dance," as the Ryzen said. Nevertheless, he gained skill with the weapons system and blasted more than one small boat out of the water.

Tamu and Bahi spent their evenings together in their citadel lodgings. There were no children to share the space with them, as Maz was in the barracks and Tahari had her own alaya, a home made of rounded domes around a central common courtyard, as many young women did. Their days were busy; Tamu continued to search the stars, while Bahi worked at the house of healers. She was busier than she had ever been, but every wounded patient she treated was a reminder that her two remaining children were at risk in this horrible war.

Chapter 8

"An untruthful person speaks lies, and as a result is short-lived. Lies are the seeds of death and despair."

~Prophecy of the Nine Grandmothers

Nesos, port city of Theralona

The bustling city was more crowded than usual. Once the call went out for sailors and laborers of all sorts, people flooded into Nesos from villages all over Theralona. Brakos had put together a substantial army, and managed to persuade the Assembly to finance his operations. He convinced the Assembly that Timur Laut planned to invade Theralona with a fleet of Sikka Manu flyers, showing them falsified log books supposedly found in the captured vehicles. He also claimed the three Sikka Manu they had acquired were stopped by his "personal army" while attempting to attack the Theralona coastline, never mentioning that he took his crew to Timur Laut to ambush and murder the defenseless ships' crews. Brakos' plans were going forward nicely.

His extensive knowledge of Timur Laut was explained by the fact that he had been an exchange student, and attended the Maga Vihar for three years before he was expelled, at that point returning to Theralona to begin his apprenticeship in the law courts. He never mentioned that he tried twice to join the Ryzen and failed. He was convinced there was secret magic known only to the Ryzen, and thought if he could acquire that knowledge he could rule both Timur Laut and Theralona.

Brakos believed he was better than his peers—stronger, smarter, more attractive, and in every way superior to everyone else. In reality, while he was well above average in size and strength, his intelligence was barely adequate for his position as a new senator, and he had only gotten that Inherited position due to his family's wealth. most people did not find his greasy yellow hair and beard attractive at all. If Brakos had been as intelligent as he thought he was, he would have seen how his attitude and appearance repelled people and modified his behavior; as it was, he attracted other less-intelligent people who longed to be important and wanted to be associated with his wealth and growing fame. They gravitated towards his movement like sharks to a bleeding carcass, scenting the possibility of personal gain. Many of his followers thought they were underappreciated in the democratic society of Theralona. Most of them couldn't vote, since they didn't own land; current law prohibited adding adult children to the ownership title of parent's homes or lands unless the parents were too ill or weak to manage it themselves. Brakos with his paid protestors and hired storytellers, who called themselves the Equality Party, gathered quite a mob of disaffected adult children who felt left out of the democratic process and wanted to force their changes through the Assembly and Senate without following the accepted method of petitions and debates. This anti-Timur Laut movement was perfect.

If they convinced the people that Timur Laut was a real enemy bent on conquest, and presented themselves as brave warriors defending their country, it was likely that a vote to extend the electorate to include all legal adults would actually pass the Assembly. Then, of course, they would vote for whomever he recommended, no more bothersome old Senators. He would stack the senate with people he could trust. the right minded ones that did what he told them too. Then they would overturn the Great Treaty and put Theralona in its proper place—ruling the world. And, of course, since by then they would be the rulers of Theralona, Brakos and his friends would rule the world and enjoy the benefits of finally being where they should be.

The general population was falling for this plan. They saw the Sikka Manu flyers Brakos presented to them as evidence of invasion attempts. It never occurred to the average voter that it was, instead, evidence of attacks on Timur Laut by Brakos himself! What kind of person would accuse someone of doing the very thing they were doing themselves? Ridiculous! Clearly, Timur Laut was violating the Great Treaty, and had broken the peace agreement. No one suspected the Brakos of manufacturing the "crisis", purely for political gain.

The people of Theralona, and especially the city of Nesos, believed everything told to them by the storytellers brakos has paid to go throughout the city and even beyond its borders. Surely the heralds wouldn't lie! And, in fact, they hadn't; their stories always began with "According to Brakos, leader of the Isos movement,…" which was perfectly true. That was exactly what Brakos had said. The heralds who repeated the news according to brakos and rode on horseback to recount it in outlying villages were careful never to say that Brakos' claims were proven, just that he and his companions were saying these things. They could prove that, if it became necessary.

In the meantime, Brakos was busy building up his army. They hadn't been able to build a working Sikka in imitation of the captured vessels; in fact, they'd been unable to do more than get the flyers to rise more than a few cubits off the ground, or over the surface of the ocean. Because they had only captured three Sikka Manu, they were forced to conduct all their raids by sea, which was possible because the Timur Laut mines where wailu kile grew were all within half a day's walk from the ocean. If there were mines further inland, Brakos didn't know about them. The three he knew about were enough.

Unfortunately, there were guards posted everywhere, and the last couple of raid attempts had been unsuccessful. They had to do something to stir the people up. Why weren't the Grandmothers of Timur Laut taking action? Didn't they realize they were being invaded? The people and Assembly of Theralona believed the story they were told; why didn't the Grandmothers believe the reverse story Brakos had fabricated? Surely they believed by now that Theralona intended to invade them?

Well, Brakos realized, it was obvious he hadn't been forceful enough. Taking three Sikka Manu and killing a few flight crews hadn't convinced them. It was becoming clear to him that he needed to do something to escalate the war. Coastal raids where no lives were lost simply weren't enough. It was up to him to take it to the next level. He called his closest companions together. They knew where the flyers came from; they'd been with him on his raids. They knew Timur Laut had not violated the Treaty, but Brakos had convinced them the story was needed in order to achieve their aims. It didn't matter if their story wasn't technically true; it was essentially true, because if a war didn't happen, the status quo of powerlessness for their group would continue. That was obviously unthinkable; they were born to rule. They were just telling a story that was true in its essence, if not factually true. Timur Laut was a danger to Theralona, because if the current situation of peace continued, Brakos and his cohort would be destroyed, and they were the best and brightest Theralona offered. Anyone with a brain could see that!

Brakos' latest plan involved raiding a fishing village further south along the coast than they had been before. As far as Brakos knew, there were no patrols that far south, so there should be no one to hinder them. They could bring their boats in close enough to send warriors in on the few gliders they had found on the Sikka; for some reason, they worked perfectly, and each Sikka Manu had three glide boards. They floated just as well over water as over land, so nine warriors could float in silently and attack a village or two, killing as many people as possible.

Brakos couldn't tell all his lieutenants his entire plan, of course—not until they were on their way. That way, anyone who objected could be pitched overboard. He thought it was unlikely that anyone would complain, since this was the logical extension of their strategy. They would leave a few people alive to report that their attackers were from Theralona, and his team was instructed to talk loudly about carrying out the orders of the Assembly. After this mission, the people of Timur Laut and their senile old Grandmothers would be convinced of the need to attack in retaliation. Once a genuine attack on Theralona happened, the Assembly would surely declare war—and who else would they appoint as commander of the armies? Who else but Brakos, who already had an army and ships at his command? It was a sure thing.

Early the next morning, he assembled his most trusted followers. They filled up three ships, the new type with two masts and huge sails. Each ship required a crew of thirty, and Brakos stationed three of his most loyal lieutenants on each ship. It would be an easy thing to slip in under cover of dusk, attack the village, and slip back out before full dark. Then they could easily navigate their way home by the stars and the light of the waxing moon. He would go with one of the teams himself, and would take charge of the raid once they were all on land.

Shortly after they set sail, one of his close friends, Miros, asked him what the purpose of the raid would be. He noticed their destination was not any of the known mining sites. Would Brakos give them their orders now?

"You'll find out the mission objective when we get there, same as everyone else," Brakos told him. "And the sailors who won't be going ashore don't need to know the rest of the plan. This is strictly for the ones who will be executing it … so to speak." He grinned, which seemed odd to Miros, but then Brakos had been getting more and more peculiar with every day.

Miros was becoming concerned that Brakos wasn't really motivated by wanting a fairer voting system; he was beginning to suspect that Brakos was aiming for personal power rather than a fair shake for everyone. If he was right … well, it would be awkward. Clearly he couldn't continue to support him, but would he have to betray an old friend to avoid committing a greater evil? Was it possible Brakos' plan involved harming innocent civilians? Up to now, only defense forces had been attacked. And certainly, it was a good thing for them to know the weapons they would fight against. Miros got into this under the belief that Timur Laut was planning an invasion, and had built up a fleet of powerful flying machines to accomplish that. However, their attempts to prod them into action and expose their real agenda had failed. Miros was beginning to wonder if there was such an agenda, after all. Perhaps it was as they said, the Sikka Manu were just left over from the War that was being used for peaceful purposes. Had Brakos been deceiving them all along? Miros didn't want to think that. Resolutely, he put the thought away and focused on watching the sailors do their job as they traveled across the ocean.

Chapter 9

"If you do not control the enemy, the enemy will control you."

~CreeVa Kau, War Chief of the Nine Tribes, Senior Commander of the Ryzen

Past midnight, and Maz was sound asleep. He became aware of something touching his foot. Still mostly asleep, he kicked out, only to have his foot grabbed.

"Ssh! Wake up! Stop kicking! Do you want me to yank off your covers the way I do in the mornings?" Lupo hissed.

Maz sat up. "What? What's going on? What are you doing here?"

"There's an emergency. We're called out. Get dressed and let's go."

Maz hurried into his uniform and vest, slipped into his sandals, and tied his hair back at the neck, asking questions the whole time.

"What kind of emergency? Who called us?"

"I met with the Grandmothers a dozen minutes ago. They told me to hurry, because the news was urgent."

"What are they doing up at this hour? And how did they get news? Patagas don't fly at night."

"A night pataga, of course. Three night patagas, actually. We use the black night patagas at night, and the regular grey colored patagas during the day. How do you not know that?"

"I've never had to send a message in the middle of the night!"

"Right. Nevertheless, we have to go. Three villages were attacked, and innocents were killed. Men, women, and children."

"Children? That's horrible!

"Yes, it is. You ready?"

"Let's go. What does Uncle always say? We have battles to fight."

They hurried out of the dormitory and walked briskly towards the Hall of Ancients. This was the domain of the Makarishi, the Nine Grandmothers. Maz tried to look casual, but it was exciting to be going to meet the unquestioned rulers of Timur Laut. The Grandmothers only interfered in the affairs of the land when the matter was extremely serious. They were silent on matters of trade, disputes between Crafts, and so forth, but they were swift to act in matters which affected the safety and well-being of the nation.

Jebal caught up to them as they reached the entrance of the Hall. The center of government was built in a traditional style, round, with seats built into the walls and a fire pit in the center of the floor. The sweet-scented smoke drifted up to the chimney hole in the roof. Halfway up the walls, a recessed dais bore a long table; nine women sat behind it, wearing different brightly colored robes, feathered crowns on their heads atop coiled silver braids.

The three men entered, stood in front and below the dais, with heads bowed and hands respectfully at waist level, palms pressed together. Maz was aware of others standing as they did, waiting to hear what the Grandmothers were going to say.

It soon became evident the Grandmothers were unhappy.

"They killed children!" said the woman sitting in the center of the line. "Children. A nine-year-old girl. A four-year-old boy. They broke into houses and dragged them out and killed them!" Her rage was such that the air around her shimmered as if it was superheated. For all Maz knew, it was. The Grandmothers were said to have strange powers. Maybe she was about to catch fire.

"We are giving this task to the Ryzen, and only the Ryzen." The shorter woman at the end spoke in the accent of the western islands, soft and musical. "Go to the villages attacked by these monsters. Use the Ryzen gifts. Find out who did this, and avenge my grandchildren."

The next woman had the clipped speech of the far north. "Go. Avenge my grandchildren."

The guttural speech of the desert lands followed as the third woman said, "Make them pay, or I will unleash the Mongwa."

Her eyes looked strangely rounded and glowing, as if the kachina spirit of the owl flared out of them, the nocturnal forward-seeing bird who was the enforcer of laws and defender of the innocent.

One after the other, the Nine Grandmothers gave the charge to the Ryzen standing before them, with accents and characteristics from every corner of the continent of Timur Laut, from the far-voyaging people of the tropical islands of the far west to the hardy folk of the northern wasteland, the hunters of the High Plains and the Spine, the cave dwellers of the Blood Mountains, the nomads of the open range, the southern fisher folk, the hunters of the rainforests, the farmers of the central valleys, and the city folk of their own northeast. All were represented, and if one was harmed, all were harmed. Coyote, Sasquatch, the Kachinas, the great manitous, all spoke through the anger of these powerful women.

Cree stepped forward, and only then did Maz realize he was there.

"The Ryzen accept this charge, noble Grandmothers. We will not fail you."

Without a command, perfectly in unison, every Ryzen clapped his hands together once, and the burst of sound was an acknowledgement by every one of them. It would be done.

"Let's go, Ryzen," Cree said in his booming voice. "We have battles to win."

Maz followed Lupo and Jebel at a fast trot as they hurried to their Sikka. They sped through the pre-flight checks by rote, secured themselves in their seats, and sounded the request for takeoff. The restraining clamps withdrew from the landing gear, they rolled forward until they cleared the shelter, then rose into the air and flew swiftly south. The three Ichaks rested securely in their brackets; Maz was still amazed at how comfortable the weapon and the capaicha that linked him to it felt when he was connected to them. They were so much a part of him that when they weren't linked, he kept wanting to reach for the connection the way his tongue might search for a missing tooth. He hadn't felt that close to his wooden staff, but then, his wooden staff didn't contain wailu kile embedded in its ends, and it wasn't connected to his mind. He even named the Ichak; he thought of his weapon as Truthbringer, though he didn't really know why. It just seemed right.

Their assigned village was the closest of the three. When they landed their Sikka, they secured it, locking down the systems to only respond to both their voices and the touch of their hands. No bandit would be able to fly off with it—not even by using their bodies to unlock the system. It only responded to living tissue and the mind-link through the capaicha. They got out of the flyer, weapons in hand.

Their backup arrived at about the same time; two more Sikka Manu with three-person crews. Lupo was the most experienced crew chief, so he took point.

A woman, clearly the acting chief of the village, approached.

"Noble Ryzen! Please help us! We have many wounded here. Some are near death. Also, we have captured one of the bandits. He is slightly wounded, but he can wait for healing."

"A captive? Excellent. We will question him. First, we must care for the wounded." Lupo turned to the backup crews. "Who has the gift of healing?"

Three of the six stepped forward. Quickly, other villagers came forward and they were shown to the house where the wounded were being cared for. Lupo promised to join them when the situation allowed.

"My healing gift is secondary, useful only for lifesaving aid. My primary gift is something else." The woman nodded; evidently she understood, which was more than Maz could say of himself. His confusion grew when Lupo turned to him.

"Maz, has your gift manifested yet?"

"Gift? What gift?"

Lupo sighed in disappointment. "I had hoped... well, never mind. Be sure to tell me when anything happens, though. We're going to need everyone's gifts when this war gets going."

"What kind of thing?"

"Anything that shows your connection to your Ichak is forming. It's different for everyone."

"Like giving it a name?"

Lupo brightened. "Yes! You've named your weapon? What's the name? Is it male or female?"

"What do you mean, male or female? It's a staff, not a person!"

"They all have personalities. What's his name?"

Maz replied without thinking. "Her name is Truthbringer."

As soon as he said it, the staff glowed. Lupo shouted for joy and raised his own staff, which was also glowing.

"Yes! Just the one we need! Hey, everyone!" he called. "We have an interrogator! Anyone else have that gift?"

One of the other Blues raised her staff. "I have Whisperer. He makes people speak even if they want to be silent."

"What other gifts do we have?"

The remaining two Ryzen, Shuka and Boro, identified their staffs as Pathfinder and Blackout. Lupo was pleased.

"You two, and Jemal with his staff Shaker. Search the village and the surrounding area. See if there's anyone hiding out. Meet back here to report at sunrise." The three acknowledged the order and left. Lupo followed the chief and gestured for Maz to do the same.

"Now, let's go see this captured raider. If he needs healing, I'll do it. I don't do much healing, because my gift hurts the patient. It saves lives, but that's all. It's a side effect of my main gift."

"What's your gift?" asked Maz.

Lupo looked him in the eye. "What's the opposite of healing?"

Maz thought for a moment. "Getting sick?"

Lupo shook his head. "Mouse, you're priceless." He held up his staff. "This is Slayer."

Maz didn't ask any more questions. Besides, they had reached the house where the captive was being held. Time for Truthbringer to do her job.

#   #   #   #   #

Miros looked up as two strangers entered the room. Like most of the people of Timur Laut, they wore their long dark hair tied back and had coppery brown skin and brown eyes. He supposed his light brown hair and grey eyes, not to mention his light, slightly tanned skin, looked strange to them. He tried to sit up, but the pain in his side from his self-inflicted slash had increased steadily through the night, and it was difficult to sit up with his hands and feet tied with ropes.

Maz placed the tip of Truthbringer against the chest of Miros.

"Name?" asked the taller, thin one, who appeared to be in charge.

"Miros son of Lagos," he answered.

"True," said the younger, more muscular man as the staff he held glowed with a cool blue light.

Hmm. A truth detector of some kind. These people definitely had better technology than his own. He resolved to stick to the truth as much as possible.

"Why are you here?" asked the tall man. His command of the kana, the trade language used by both nations, was good, although he had a bit of an accent.

"Me, or the group I was with?"

"Both."

"First, then, the group I was with is trying to start a war."

"True."

"I'm here because I'm an idiot. I trusted foolishly."

"Also true."

"Tell your story, from the beginning, slowly."

"I'll tell you everything, but first, can I get this wound treated?"

"It's not life threatening. Talk first. Healing after."

Miros didn't blame them for their priorities. He would do the same thing in their place.

"The leader is Senator Brakos son of Oris. I've known Brakos since we were students at the Lyceum, before he went to your country as a student. He was different then, or maybe I just didn't see it. I thought we were friends, but now I don't think he has friends, only tools to use in his plan to rule over everything."

"Everything? That's a big plan. How does he think he's going to do that?"

"The short answer is to start a war between Theralona and Timur Laut, win the war, get himself named warlord or something, pass new voting laws in Assembly, declare himself head of the Senate, and get everything under his control and eventually somehow become king. I didn't figure it out until very recently. I honestly thought he believed we were defending ourselves against the threat of war."

A purple light shone from the young man's staff.

"Break those statements apart. Does this Brakos fellow want to rule the world?"

"Yes. I believe so, anyway."

Blue light.

"Does he believe Timur Laut is a threat?"

"To his plan, yes. To Theralona, no."

Blue, again.

"Do you believe Timur Laut is a threat to Theralona?"

"Well... in a way... maybe."

The light from the staff turned red.

Fascinating. That proved Miros' theory that the device sensed the speaker's belief, not just the facts.

"I think I might have believed him at first, but I no longer do."

Purple.

"I guess I always knew it was a lie, but I wanted to believe him in spite of my better judgement."

Blue.

"Now we're getting somewhere. Just tell your story. If Truthbringer doesn't like it, we'll back up and find where we went off the pathway. Got it?"

"Yes, I understand. So, Brakos has been getting crazier for years. He claims people in flying discs attacked us and he had to kill them in self-defense. The bodies magically disappeared."

Blue.

"It looks like he really said that. In fact, he came here, stole the ships, and murdered the crew." The questioner was calm, but Miros could tell it was through self-control and not a lack of emotion.

"Including my brother," said the younger man, with clenched teeth.

"I'm sorry that happened," said Miros. "I didn't know for sure, but I suspected his story was fake."

Blue light. "Go on."

"He has been trying to get the vote for non-property owners. He thinks they would vote for his policies. He wants to raise taxes on property, on sale of goods, on profits. Property owners won't vote for that. He wants to control the voters by making them dependent on the government for their needs. It's complicated, and it's all about political power. He needed an enemy, so he manufactured one. He has the Assembly almost convinced that Timur Laut is planning to invade Theralona, enslave our people, and take our resources."

Blue light.

The tall man said some things that Miros figured weren't suitable for translation.

"Look, Miros, I'm going to heal that slash. How did you get it, anyway?"

"I did it myself, with my kopis."

"Kopis?"

"Long knife. It wasn't very smart, but I needed a way to stay behind, and I wasn't going to kill any of your people. I needed a reason to be bloody and fake unconsciousness. I knew Brakos would leave me behind if I looked badly hurt."

"I think that was very smart. My name is Lupo. This is Maz. I think we'll bring you back to talk to the Grandmothers."

"Grandmothers?"

"Our land is governed by a council of Senhani and Craftmasters, for the day to day business, but for serious matters like national defense we look to the Nine Grandmothers, wise women from each region who have a stake in the future through their grandchildren. They all have actual descendants, but in a spiritual sense we are all their grandchildren." It was the one called Maz who explained this to Miros, and he clearly cared deeply about the matter.

"My father is a Senhan. His discipline is the study of the stars. My uncle is a Craftmaster, representing the Farmers' Craft. We don't need to enslave anyone to have a prosperous economy. That's a ridiculous idea. Freedom and hard work bring prosperity."

"And the Grandmothers..."

"They care about the future. They have a long view. The Senhani and the Crafthall look to the present," said the tall one... Lupo.

"I want to meet these Grandmothers," Miros said.

Blue.

Chapter 10

"A warrior must have a firm conviction in the pursuit of goodness through the virtues of love, faith, charity, and honesty, even at the risk of one's own life."

~ Tome of the Ryzen

Nesos City, Theralona

"We have a visitor. It's not good, brothers."

Dalini was clearly upset, which was not usual for him. The normally calm, logical Ryzen was breathing just a little too fast, his eyes glancing around the room a little too nervously. The locals wouldn't notice, but his fellow Ryzen did.

They were having an emergency meeting in the private tower that was functionally the Timur Laut embassy. It rose above Nesos City, providing a place where no listening ears could overhear anything they had to say. Dalini and his fellow pilot-ambassadors, Sidu and Matay, had lived among the Theralonians for nearly a dozen years. They had learned to read the culture, and they were all concerned about the feeling in the streets against their homeland. Dalini, however, was even more concerned. The content of the message he received that morning was the source of the concern.

"The visitors, two Ryzen, arrived before sunrise with a message from War Chief Cree," he told them. "We've been recalled, sir. We're expected in Timur Laut by sunset. There were raids on villages last night. Innocent fishing villages, and people were killed. Murdered. Old men, women, and children. They think the death toll will be over three dozen unless the healers are unusually skillful. Apparently it's the work of this Brakos fellow, the one that's campaigning for the vote for the poor. He claims we attacked their coast, and supposedly has three Sikka Manu he's captured to prove it. But the Clerk's message said the crews of the Sikka Manu were found. Their bodies were hidden near the mines. That was the motive; get hold of the Sikka Manu and some wailu kile. Our brothers and sisters were murdered by Brakos and his armies. And they're blaming our people for it!"

"Calm yourself, brother. We can get out of the city on a moment's notice, if need be. I've spoken with the visitors; they took our Sikka to the henge for refueling. They left theirs for us to follow them as soon as possible. It's fully charged, too. We'll be all set for the trip. All the way back to the landing field without a refueling. We just have to grab our underwear and tooth cleaners and go. Unless you've been slacking, you should have your fly-bag packed and ready at all times, per the rules."

"But… we have friends…"

"Sidu, you know he's fussing about leaving the pretty little red haired girl behind," said Matay.

"That's right," said Sidu. "Dalini forgets himself when she's around. Sorry, friend, but you don't have time for a last snuggle."

"Shut up already. I know. And, yes, my bag is ready. We have to go, that's clear. I don't have to be happy about it." Dalini took a deep breath; the brief bout of joking around with his captain had relaxed him, as Matay knew it would. He was very good with his subordinates, making sure they never felt like subordinates but like valued teammates—always knowing, however, that Matay was in charge. He was the senior Ryzen in Theralona, and watched his crew as carefully as a protective mama bear with two rowdy cubs.

"I've been thinking about this, too, boys," Matay said. "I don't want to give any warning, or even send a formal farewell letter. We'll just go. Now. With a little good fortune, they won't even know we're gone until the war is over."

"War?" asked Sidu, surprised.

"That's what I'm reading," Matay told him. I had a message myself, in the packet our brothers brought. The Grandmothers are on the point of calling for war. The War Chief believes the time for diplomacy is over. Let's get our bags and go to the roof. We fly."

Just then, sounds reached the tower room; heavy footsteps coming up the stairs.

"Sounds like we'll get to have a little fun before we leave," Matay said as he smiled at his Blues. "Get ready."

All three picked up their Ichaks and their capaicha from the case holding them and took up positions by the entry.

The door burst open as a dozen heavily armed soldiers with long knives and spears, members of Brakos' personal guard, began to rush through the door. A powerful strike from Sidu's staff hit the first one through square in the face, sending him reeling back helmet flying off into the man behind him, who stumbled and fell. The strike left him with a smashed and broken nose, the blood gushing out before he could open his eyes to see Sidu aiming another overhead strike to the top of his head; it connected, cracking his skull with an audible pop. He fell. The second guard behind him got back up, narrowly avoiding being knocked over a second time. As he stood, confused, an upward strike from Danili's staff connected with his chin and launched the guard off his feet nearly four hands into the air, shattering his jaw in the process. He landed backwards head first on the stone floor, unconscious. Matay watched out of the corner of his eyes with some pride as his brothers effortlessly dismantled the first wave of guards. From his position to the left of the entrance, he was in a good position to intercept the next pair of guards that broke through and headed in his direction. The two right behind broke off and headed towards Sidu.

With blinding speed Matay swung low with the repulsion power and swept both the guards legs out from under them, his staff still over a forearm's distance away. They lay, stunned, as

Matay stepped in with head strikes to one, then the other, taking both out of the fight. The guard on the right flank lunged at Sidu with his spear, and Sidu parried it to the side and grabbed it with his left hand, bringing up his Ichak to block a sword strike from the next guard. Sidu twisted the staff to disarm the attacker, turning it end-first to send a power strike from his Ichak, nicknamed the Sickness, directly to his midsection. The guard dropped to his knees and began vomiting all over the floor.

Danili evaded a thrown spear that whizzed by his head as he turned to face two more guards. The first, who had thrown the spear, took a swing at him with a long bladed, drop point knife aimed at his neck. Danili deftly blocked the knife with his Ichak, kneed the guard in the groin, and head butted his nose; seeing stars, the guard thrashed wildly, swinging his long knife as the guard behind him rushed at Danili.

Matay caught the guard's movement in his peripheral vision; as soon as he dispatched his two he turned, spun around, and jabbed the tip of his Ichak, the Darkness, into the back of the guard charging Danili, with an extra charge of repelling force. The guard flew right past him and into the wall across the room, clearly unable to see as he waved his arms frantically around. Sidu was still holding the first guard's spear as the guard struggled to free it, but when his other attacker was dispatched he touched the guard on the cheek with his Ichak. The guard let go of the spear and fell to the ground, vomiting uncontrollably. The four remaining guards in the attack force wisely decided not to continue the attack. They shouted, turned around and ran away to get reinforcements.

"Good work, boys!" Matay said. "Time to go." He headed back into the tower room.

Danili followed, with a slight look of disappointment. "You got to use Darkness and Sickness but I didn't get to use Heavyweight".

"You could have used it instead of that head butt, you have options, you don't always need to smash things with your head" said Sidu laughing and shaking his head at the same time.

"Next time, Danili. For now, let's grab our bags and fly." The three gathered up their bags, ready as per regulations.

Matay continued, "Good thing we're not staying here, or you would be cleaning up all that vomit, Sidu!"

All three Ryzen laughed, glad to have survived that one unscathed. They climbed the stairs to the roof, got in the waiting Sikka and lifted off.

An hour past midday, Matay and his crew reached the shores of Timur Laut. Tambak City was just a short flight further inland, and they would give their report to War Chief Cree and, perhaps, the Grandmothers themselves. A dozen years as diplomats had prepared them for the intensity of the moments ahead. They were about to meet the people from whom they received their orders.

The peaceful shoreline below gave way to forested areas of rich green, followed by cultivated fields and scattered farmhouses. Finally, they reached the city with its landmarks; the Pyramid of the Moon, the buildings of the Maga Vihar , the Ryzen home base and flying field, and right in the center, next to the flying field, the Sacred Mound rising up to the Circle of the Sun, with the amplifying serpentine paths weaving around the mound from its base to the peak where the Temple Rock drew all eyes for miles around. On festival days, the fires lit on the Rock could be seen for half a dozen miles.

They flew to the field at the edge of the mound, where one of the paths led to a charging station. They looked to the ground where Ryzen were waiting for them, found a vacant spot, hovered for a moment, and descended. They shut down the flyer, grabbed their fly-bags and Ichaks, and walked to the waiting group.

War Chief Cree was there to meet them, which was an unexpected honor. He was impressive in his long brown vest, wide fur collar, a deep gorget of silver mesh inlaid with symbols of his office around his neck, fur epaulets over his shoulders, a helmet of silver with turquoise stones and white feathers on his head. He wore a black tunic and calf length kilt under the brown vest, indicating his new status as a provisional Sage, and his heavy leather sandals were fastened with silver buckles. The three diplomats were in awe. The outfit was normally a bit too fancy for crees liking but as war chief he is expected to dress and carry himself a certain way for formal meetings such as this.

"Welcome back, boys! I'll bet you have quite a story to tell! They've got baths ready for you, and some food. Go ahead and get freshened up, have a quick bite to eat, and we'll meet in the conference room so you can tell me your story. We're meeting with the Grandmothers after the evening meal, and we need to put all our information together so we can present it to them. I wanted to see for myself that you're alright."

"Thank you, sir. It's an honor to meet you." Matay bowed, and his crew did likewise. his crew stepped up and bowed; they gestured for the diplomats to follow. They did so, and soon were comfortably settled in a guest room in the Hall of Visitors, adjacent to the Ryzen public rooms.

"Nice," commented Dalini as they walked into the rooms they'd been given.

"Better than a dormitory," agreed Sidu, looking around. The guest quarters had a large sitting room with comfortable benches and chairs and a large table laden with fruit, bread, and meats. To one side was a hygiene chamber with several bathing tubs, curtained commodes, and hand washing stations with water spigots. On further investigation, they found a sleeping chamber with half a dozen comfortable looking beds. Clothing was stacked on shelves against the wall, no doubt for visitors who arrived without a change of clothing.

They bathed quickly, dressed, ate some food and drank kafi. There was chocolate available, but they all wanted the additional energy obtained from the unique blend of kafi and green Yerba tea favored by the Ryzen. They finished just as a knock on the door preceded the entry of their escorts. It was time to tell their stories.

#   #   #   #   #

The conference room was crowded. War Chief Cree presided, at the head of a horseshoe shaped table. In the middle of the horseshoe, a tall, narrow table waited, a single pitcher and cup resting on its surface. Pitchers of water and pottery cups sat at intervals around the horseshoe table. As Matay, Sidu and Dalini entered with their escorts, the noise level in the room decreased. They were soon seated at one end of the horseshoe; at the other was a yellow-haired man in a loose white tunic, worn with the shawl known in Theralona as a chiton.

'What's a Theralonian doing here?' wondered Matay. 'Is he a spy or a prisoner?'

"Be seated," said the Ryzen in blue feathers who stood at the narrow central table and appeared to be acting as aide to the War Chief. "We will hear all of your reports in due time."

When everyone was seated, he consulted a scroll on the table in front of him. It was well-rubbed parchment, probably reused over and over by various clerks.

"Headwoman Niwota," he said. "Come forward and be heard by the War Chief."

A tall woman stepped up to the table and stood facing the War Chief. She bowed, and he raised a hand in acknowledgment.

"I come today to speak of the great injury done to my village,". she said. "Men of Theralona crept into my village by night, with big knives in their hands, and they broke into people's homes and began killing them without cause. Men, women, children, they killed anyone who was in their path. They murdered my people! They were shouting, in the kana language, "For the glory of the Assembly and the people of Theralona!"

The War Chief raised an eyebrow.

"They were shouting in kana, not Helana? How strange. It's as if they were shouting to the village, not to their own gang. Never mind; continue."

"Sir, I know it was in kana, the trade language. I am familiar with kana because I work with trading ships from many countries and we all must learn the kana. I don't know this Helana and would not have understood if they shouted my own name in it!"

"You are correct, Headwoman. What you say confirms my suspicion. How were they driven off?"

"Someone rang a brass gong on their front porch, and it woke everyone. More gongs sounded. By that time, the whole village was awake. We shouted and beat the bandits with sticks, and those who had bolo knives and pira swords attacked them as well. There were five of them against the entire village of a dozen dozen adults and twice that many children. Yes, even the children fought them with sticks and with brooms. We captured one of them. There he sits, right there! I claim my right to his skin to make a mat to wipe my feet on!

"I will consider your request, Headwoman. Thank you. ". At the War Chief's words, the woman bowed and returned to her seat.

The blue feathered Ryzen raised his voice. "We have heard the testimony of Niwota, Headwoman of Wanusa village. Who speaks for Anaki village?"

A young boy about a dozen years old rose from his seat and walked to the speakers' table.

"I am Yoshi, and I am here because my father is headman of Anaki. If he is still living; he was not doing well when I left."

The War Chief looked at his aide. "Were healers sent to this village?"

"Yes, sir. They had good hopes for the headman's recovery."

"Very well. You may speak, Yoshi. Tell me what happened."

The boy's testimony was like the headwoman's; armed bandits breaking into homes, yelling about the Assembly and Theralona. All the bandits ran away when the villagers were roused and disappeared.

Last, the elderly headman from Teki gave his testimony. His name was Motu, and he was furious at the bandits who invaded his village. He had killed one with his bare hands, slamming the bandit's head into a stone wall. Four bandits had attacked him and ran away when their compatriot fell. They had backed him against the wall, but he fought hard and they couldn't overpower him.

"Cowards! I would have killed them all if they hadn't run away. I don't run so fast anymore," he admitted. "I'm eight dozen years old and my knees bother me."

"I could use your help encouraging new recruits," the War Chief said. "You saved your village. Not one life was lost in Teki except for the bandit."

"That's right, sir. A couple of the boys were knocked out, and one took a knife slash to his leg, but not a bad wound. They were up and chasing the bandits almost right away. I've trained them well." He went on to explain that these "boys" were grandfathers and were starting to slow down a bit, or they would have caught the bandits.

"You bring honor to your village, friend Motu. Join me at my table tonight for dinner. I'd like to hear more about your training methods. We can share stories. Now I want to hear from the one who didn't get away. Bring the prisoner to the speakers' table."

Miros stepped up to the table, his arms bound in front of him. He faced the War Chief and bowed respectfully.

"So, Theralonian. What do you have to say for yourself? You've heard the testimony. Is it true? Did your bandits attack peaceful villagers?"

"Yes, sir, the villagers were attacked. But the bandits are not mine. I played dead so I would be left behind. I know what Brakos is planning, and I want no part of it."

"You would betray your country?"

"Never, sir! It is Brakos who is betraying our people. I am betraying no one. I owe Brakos no loyalty, because he is himself a traitor."

"Explain."

Miros did so, eloquently. He told of his gradual disillusionment with his old school friend, and his realization that Brakos was planning to overthrow the elected government of Theralona and replace it with a monarchy with himself at the top. He described the three Sikka Manu stolen by Brakos and his gangs, and how he came to disbelieve the story that they were captured following raids on Theralonian villages.

"So your Assembly believes our people attacked you first?"

"Some of them do, sir. They have no information to the contrary. They were presented with Brakos' claims, and took them at face value. They saw three Sikka Manu, and believed what he said. Why should they not? Brakos has been careful. I believed him at first, but I eventually began to see him for what he truly is. I wanted no part of killing innocents, and I was horrified when he revealed his plan to us only after we were about to launch the attack. I couldn't stop him alone, so I wounded myself and pretended to be unconscious. Brakos doesn't bother to carry dead weight. I'm thankful he didn't decide to run me through with a spear to prove I was really dead!"

"What did you hope to gain by pretending to be unconscious?"

"I hoped to do exactly as I am doing, sir; telling the truth to the War Chief of Timur Laut. I don't want war, especially not to satisfy one man's thirst for power. If I am to be killed for it, it will be worth it if I can prevent a war."

"Why should I believe you?"

"Do you have means of detecting the truth, sir?"

"As it happens, I do. Maz, bring your gift here."

The young man named Maz stepped forward, his Ichak, Truthbringer, in hand. Miros recognized it from his questioning in the house back in the village. Maz touched the staff to Miros' chest.

"This is Truthbringer," he said to Miros. "It has the power to discern truth and lies. Tell me again. Is everything you've told us the absolute truth?" he asked in a stern voice.

"It is absolutely true," said Miros.

Truthbringer glowed with a blue light.

"The blue light means Truthbringer senses truth in what this man says," said Maz. "Truthbringer can not be deceived. What he says is proven to be true by the arts of the Ryzen."

"So be it," said the War Chief. "The prisoner may be seated. We will deal with your fate later. Now, let the ambassador to Theralona and his aides come forward to give their testimony."

Matay, Sidu and Dalini stepped forward, bowed, and stood at attention at the speaker's table.

"Ambassador Matay Ilu, Ryzen Sidu and Dalini, what can you tell us about this situation that will enlighten us and improve our understanding of the deceptions and violence practiced against our nation?"

"War Chief, I didn't understand some of my own information until just now, when I listened to Miros here. This is what happened. I heard about the supposed raids by Sikka Manu on the Theralonian coast. I didn't believe it. But I didn't know how they got hold of our Ryzen craft. That is why I dispatched an urgent message to the Sage as soon as I found out. We had ours, but it was kept hidden at the top of our tower of course. Protection of the ancient knowledge is always a top priority in any Ryzen mission, diplomatic or otherwise, sir. no one in Nesos City outside the three of us knew we had a Sikka. We didn't take it out except at night to recharge at the secret henge. The henges are like our serpent mounds, and can be used to recharge our vehicles.

"I'm aware of that, Ambassador Matay."

"Yes, sir. When I heard this Barkos had three Sikka Manu, I became concerned and began looking for where he had them hidden. We can track them when they are in use but when they are powered down we can not. From what I could tell, his political group wanted to change the voting rules while the senate has control of the nation until the boy king is of age. They thought it would be easier to take power and easier to manipulate people by promising them food and money without the need to work, which is ridiculous. But in their cities, the poor who own no property outnumber those who own land and homes. In the countryside, the reverse is true, but the power is in the large cities. If beggars can vote themselves free food, they can also be controlled by those who hand out the food. The threat of losing a handout keeps them doing what the manipulators want them to do. This Brakos is devious and very disturbed. He studied here at the Academy and tried to join the Ryzen. He wants access to the ancient knowledge. He failed twice; I think any Ryzen here can guess at some of the places he failed. No one who is only looking out for himself will ever become a Ryzen.

"Knowing there was something deeply wrong, I tried to get the Sikka Manu out of his hands. I went to a contact I have in the Theralonain Assembly two days ago to ask them for information on our stolen property. They refused, and it was then I heard the entire book of lies Brakos had been spreading. Supposedly, we will be sending a fleet to conquer and enslave them, and there are those in their Assembly who believe this! My crew and I were about to begin searching his family's warehouses for the Sikka Manu when we got the word that we had been recalled, I suspect that is where he is hiding them. He must have heard about my inquiry at the assembly because he sent some of his friends to give us a going away party before we left. Sir, Brakos has the people in the street on his side, and the question of expanding the vote is before the Assembly in three days. There is a good chance it will pass. I believe he will make another move before that vote happens. The couriers who brought us the message said they had another stop to make. Is Brakos making trouble somewhere else?"

"Ambassador, thank you for your report and your service to our Order, I trust you and your men are unhurt from your- going away party?"

"Yes, sir! Not a scratch!", Matay announced proudly.

Cree continued. "Good, I believe I am ready to take a recommendation to the Grandmothers. I want you and Miros to hold yourselves ready to speak to the Grandmothers if they ask for you. The rest may go, relax, rest, refresh yourselves. Dinner will be prepared for you, and you will have accommodations here in Ryzen headquarters. We will see you returned to your homes tomorrow."

The War Chief stood. The Ryzen at the center table informed the group that they were dismissed. Matay and his crew remained behind to see what was going to happen next.

They did meet the Grandmothers, and answered their questions. Then, there was time for a rest in their rooms until dinner, when they hoped to meet with the War Chief again.

While the diplomats and villagers rested, the Sages and War Chief Cree, along with Lupo and Maz by invitation, were honored to participate in a ceremony with the Grandmothers. It was a ceremony reserved for serious proclamations and decisions; it was not often that anyone but the Grandmothers themselves participated in a sweating ceremony. Lupo and Maz waited with Cree in his chambers for the necessary preparations.

First, assistants brought them loose sleeveless robes, worn unbelted, long enough to cover their knees. They were a bright yellow color. Barefoot, they walked in these loose robes through a covered walkway to a private chamber in the Grandmothers' Hall.

It was a sweat lodge, with a huge fire built up in the middle. There were rocks to sit on around the fire. Buckets of water with ladles were within reach. Silently, everyone was invited to sit. The Nine Grandmothers entered, also dressed in yellow sleeveless robes. They wore no shoes, headgear, or jewelry. One by one, the Grandmothers tossed herbs into the fire, making the smoke extremely pungent but not unpleasant. Cree recognized a mix of many different odors burning in the fire, this was the dreamwalker ceremony. The Grandmothers joined them on the rocks.

As the heat rose, sweat ran down their faces and backs. Following the Grandmothers' lead, Cree and the younger men poured dippers of water over their heads to wash away the salt that poured out in the sweat. The Grandmothers began to chant in an ancient language.

It seemed to Cree that he saw things in the smoke. Bloody battles, with thousands upon thousands killed, of every nation in the world. He also saw men put in holding chambers, and in those visions there was no war. Then he saw waves of water sweeping over the land, submerging the coastal cities; he saw earthquakes; he saw the sky falling. He saw their people in boats, sailing west; he saw the Theralonians fleeing in fear, heading east from their homeland. These visions confused him; were they predictions of the future? Visions of what must be, or what might be? Were they alternatives of war and peace, that they might choose between? And what was the falling sky?

After a while the visions faded. Cree washed off the residue of sweat. No one spoke. One by one the grandmothers laid their hands on him and on his companions. He knew what they wanted him to do, and what edict he must publish in their name. They left, and when they were gone he stood, motioned to the other two to join him, and returned to his chamber for another bath and fresh clothing. It was almost time for dinner.

After dinner, Cree went to his writing room. Taking a large sheet of fiber paper, he settled down at his desk to begin a document that would set the course of the nation in the immediate future.

By order of War Chief Cree

We are in dangerous times. Our nation has been falsely accused of deeds that have caused the loss of life and property by a cowardly dishonorable individual. These actions were not authorized by the nation of The Theralonians as we were led to believe but by a single individual. There will be no direct retaliation against Theralonia unless provoked.

The following orders are to be effective immediately.

1. All Ryzen in the region to be recalled to Timur Laut.

2. Minimum Air patrol size: Three Sikka Manu.

3. Minimum ground team size: Six Ryzen, full battle gear at all times.

4. Protect the ancient technology at all costs.

• Primary mission: Recover the ancient technology

• Secondary mission: Protect all Tribes and Villages from attack. Capture or kill Brakos of Nesos

First order: plan a way to contact the Council of Nesos and provide evidence of the treachery by Brakos. Then obtain the whereabouts of Brakos and plan of attack, with or without the help of the council of Nesos.

Ryzen may attack on sight, Attack when attacked or when an others safety is compromised or to prevent an attack and in accordance with the mission.

Cree wrote long into the night, making corrections and re-copying until it was perfect.

Chapter 11

"Ego, is the most dangerous enemy to humans; you must master yourself before you can master your enemy."

From the Tome of the Ryzen

The long, sleek ship sped towards the large Eastern continent. Just ahead of them was the country of Tenifra, notable for its mountain ranges that stood seven thousand cubits high. The highest mountain of all was a two-hour journey inland; it was the Teid, looming above the rest in the dim light of the setting sun. At the base of the Teid were villages and rich farmlands. Brakos thought they would be easy prey once the sun was down and people were relaxing from their evening meal.

His troops followed his orders unquestioningly. Just the day before, the Assembly agreed to present the bill on voting rights to the people in three days. Brakos' men could see that his plans were coming to fruition. He was clearly a leader to follow. Even when his orders were strange, they were carried out in every detail. So, on his ship, everyone from the oarsmen to the warriors had coppery brown painted skin, colored with a potion made from walnut juice. Their hair was dark brown or black, colored with the same stain mixed with squid ink. They wore Theralonian-style tunics and chitons, and the knee-high sandals popular in Nesos City. Anyone would think they were people of Timur Laut, unless they looked closely and saw the color of their eyes. Few of them had brown eyes, and the blue and grey so common in Theralona were simply not seen in Timur Laut. It didn't matter; those who noticed would not live to tell about it. This raid would be the last straw in Brakos' campaign to get the Assembly to declare war on Timur Laut.

They waded in to shore from the shallow-keeled boat. The sail was furled, to keep it stable and at anchor. The oarsmen remained at their posts, chained to prevent them from jumping overboard to follow the song of the Sirens, which everyone knew were a risk in the eastern sea. This continent was home to many dangers and mysteries, and after this raid, the men hoped they would not have to make additional journeys to this frightful land, home of the legendary blue-painted red-haired people and the terrifying Grendels of the North. Sailors told stories around the fire about the people of the East, who were apparently all insane. The oarsmen were glad to stay on the boat; the warriors were not happy to be going ashore, but they were willing to follow Brakos anywhere.

Their feet touched dry land. Hoping the stain hadn't washed off their feet and lower legs, Brakos led the men inland towards the nearest village. He had taught them a few battle cries in the language of Timur Laut. "For the Ryzen!" was one, and "The Glory of the Grandmothers!" was another. No one would understand what they said, but the survivors would probably be able to repeat it well enough for those who investigated to conclude that Timur Laut was behind the raid. He also had some of the men shout the same thing in kana, just to be certain the message was received. Short of carrying signs that said "We are from Timur Laut", that was the best he thought they could do.

Less than two hours later, the fires of the first village came in sight. Creeping quietly, they went in pairs, kicking in the doors of the houses and slashing indiscriminately with their curved knives and bolo slashers, copied from Brakos' memory of blade training at the Academy. Here, too, the survivors would be able to tell what they had seen and point the finger squarely at the hated Ryzen's domain. Brakos knew there were Ryzen ambassadors in every land, but strangers were always feared, weren't they? This would just prove what the local people had always suspected. It was a brilliant plan.

Within an hour, Brakos whistled the signal to return. Bloodied and tired, they straggled back, slipped into the underbrush and headed for shore. He did a head count, and three out of the fifteen he brought with him weren't there. They could stay behind; they were either dead or soon would be, at the mercy of angry villagers. He'd lost Miros in last week's raid on the Timur Laut coast, but he was starting to have doubts about Miros loyalty anyway. No loss. These three were the same; if they couldn't overwhelm a village full of farmers, what good were they in a revolution? Tired and thirsty, they pushed on to the shore, then washed the blood off in the water and waded to the welcome sight of the boat's sail unfurling as they prepared to weigh anchor and head for home. Brakos had a successful day.

#   #   #   #   #

Guayota Cor, the capital city of Tenifra, was unusually subdued that morning. The news heralds that had been informed by Brakos of what had happened began calling the news from every corner; crowds gathered to hear the latest news. It was the most disturbing news they'd heard in many years.

The old ones remembered the war; battles on each of the nine continents, with the coasts suffering most of all. Tenifra was hard hit in that war, and it was still spoken about as a time of terror and hardship. The old ones said it began like this, with raids on coastal villages, then moving to attacks on major cities, eventually covering the known world. Thirty years had gone by, and people spoke as if it were yesterday. Fear of Timur Laut ran high; in the war, they rediscovered their flying machines and power wands just in the last days of the war, and the effects were so terrible that the nations all surrendered. People were surprised that Timur Laut didn't want to rule, but to be left alone; the leaders of Theralona and the nations of the northeastern continent, Pangeos, hurried to accept their peace terms, which were astoundingly mild. But now, if they were starting it up again, who could stand against them? It would be devastating.

In the Hall of Chiefs, the leaders of all the villages assembled. The princess of Tenifra presided over the group; she was young for this position, having been a babe in arms when the last war ended, but her father died young after an accident, getting gored in the back on a boar hunt. Koakoula was crowned princess at barely fourteen years of age, and now was two and thirty. She was a good leader, and the city flourished under her guidance.

She raised her hand, and the chiefs in the room fell silent.

"Brothers and sisters, let us not be so quick to accept the reports as true. We can believe something happened, but the reasons are questionable. Someone attacked our coastline. The village of Preseida is in anguish; more than five and twenty murdered in their beds, or at least in their homes when they expected no danger. But this is not what Timur Laut does. They work openly, and I would have received demands before any hostilities. All I have had is words of friendship. I will question their ambassador here, before you all. I require you to ask questions courteously, honoring this hall. Are we in accord?"

"Yes, Princess!" they all agreed with one voice.

"Bring the ambassador in," she ordered.

A Ryzen in his formal dress, with a long brown vest entered, his reddish brown hair cut short to the jawline in imitation of local fashion with a well trimmed short beard. He was of lighter skin than was common from Timur Laut, but then, not all Ryzen were from Timur Laut. His emerald green eyes looked puzzled, but not afraid.

"Greetings, Princess Koakoula." He bowed formally in the style of his people, then made a sweeping bow after the custom of the land he had lived in for a dozen years as Ambassador.

"Greetings, Ambassador Lugh," said the princess.

"As always, it is an honor to see you," replied the Ryzen. "But I must say I am puzzled. Have I been called because of the rumors I hear in the streets? I speak to you frankly, as a man of honor. Do your people believe this slander?"

"You killed my father!" shouted one chief from the crowd.

"I have killed no one. I did not fight in the war, as I was still a child of barely a dozen years. I have learned the fighting arts, but I swear to you I have killed no man, woman or child in all my life. I kill animals for food, but I do not eat people; why should I kill them?" Lugh smiled, hoping a bit of levity would lessen the tension.

"Dog! You mock me! Prepare to die!" The chief launched a javelin at the Ryzen, who caught it in his hand without breaking eye contact with the princess. The chiefs gasped at this demonstration of skill.

"Witchcraft!" cried the same man, a chief named Ingo from the village of Matoya. "See, he catches my javelin with his bare hands! Witchcraft!"

The princess spoke. "I could have done the same, Ingo. It is not so difficult. My personal combat instructor taught me to catch flying objects before I was fourteen, when my father lived. He enjoyed watching me perform. But why have you brought a weapon into my hall?" Her voice was deceptively calm.

"For just a thing as this, Princess. Lies from our enemy!"

"So you would kill him before we can learn anything from him? How does that serve our people?"

"If I may ask a question, princess?" asked Lugh, softly.

"Yes, of course, Ambassador, if it is relevant."

"I think it may be. Tell me, Chief Ingo, does the name Brakos mean anything to you?"

It did not require a Ryzen gift to see that the chief had heard the name. He turned even whiter than usual. He looked around, obviously planning his escape, when a glance from the princess had two guards at the chief's side, their hands on his shoulders.

"Ingo, I see this name means something to you. Tell us who he is."

"A tradesman from Theralona, that's all I know, Princess," the man answered. "He… he… "

"Don't waste time thinking up lies, Ingo. I don't need magic powers to see there is more to this than just a tradesman. Ambassador, will you say more?"

"I will, Princess. This Brakos is a Theraloanian Senator." At the horrified gasps from the crowd, Lugh maintained an emotionless face.

"Yes, he is one who seeks political power. He has brought a measure before their people to allow any man to vote on matters of law. According to rumor, he has aspirations of becoming King. He is popular with the common folk, and they think it would be a good thing to restore the old rule of kings to their country. This Brakos promises free food and housing, to be paid for by heavy taxes on landowners and merchants."

"But what does this have to do with the attack? Surely there are no Theralonian landowners there!" The Princess leaned forward, her interest fully captured.

"He wishes to be appointed Commander of the Armies in a war against Timur Laut," the ambassador said. "He attended the Academy and claims to be skilled in warfare, and he has a fleet of ships at his disposal since his family has built Theraloanin warships for seven generations. It is very likely the Assembly would appoint him to that position following a declaration of war."

"Why have we been told nothing of this man until now?"

"I apologize, Princess. I thought him unimportant, a foolish Theralonian politician. I did not realize until recently that their Assembly was taking him seriously. I received word that villages in Timur Laut were raided at night, by people in Theralonian attire shouting about the glory of the Assembly. The Assembly ordered no such raids; I received a message last night. One of the raiders was questioned and had much information to give. People are dying on both sides for this man's political ambitions."

"Clearly, we can take no action until the matter is resolved. Ambassador, please be my guest in this hall until…"

There was a disturbance at the door.

"The Princess must see this!"

Koakoula turned and gestured. "Bring it here, whatever it is."

An old woman entered, followed by two younger women dragging a man in a torn tunic.

The old woman stared at the princess in silence unsure of what to say,

"Well, then. you may speak freely here."

The woman spoke, encouraged by the courtesy of the princess. "My assistants were tending to this wounded man, one of the bandits left behind. The other two died, but this one lives. They were washing him, and the color came off! See!"

It was true. The women dragged the prisoner in front of the Princess. His torn tunic showed areas of very white skin underneath, and the upper legs and arms, which normally did not show with his clothing intact, were a brindled brown and beige mixture as the dark color dripped off, obviously thanks to the bathing efforts of the furious women.

"This man is no more from Timur Laut than I am," insisted the old woman. "Look how pale he is! He's from Theralona, or from the Waikin lands to the north. His hair is false, too!" she said as she pulled a wig off his head. The hair underneath was straw-colored, and when he raised his eyes everyone could see they were blue.

"What is this deception, bandit?" the princess asked the man.

"I just follows orders, that's all I does." The prisoner was clearly afraid of the women, as he kept glancing at them, his expression one of terror.

"Where are you from, bandit?"

"I's from Nesos City, sir. I growed up on the docks. I's a right good sailor, and I can row faster nor most, I swears it. Would you be needing an oarsman, sir? I doesn't want to go back home now." "Why wouldn't you want to go home?" asked the princess. "I doesn't want to work for Brakos and have to wear paint and a wig and kill children no more, no I doesn't, It were Brakos' orders. He told us to do this. I dunno why. I just do what I's told, but if I goes back he will kill me."

"You may not be as simple as you seem, but I will not have a job for you. It's to the jail cells for you, and if you answer well, you shall have supper. If you answer poorly, you shall be supper for the seabirds. Take him away!" The Princess commanded. "Let the guards question him carefully. Don't kill him, we want him alive," She added.

"Well," he said to the group. "This was interesting. It appears Brakos is, indeed, setting nation against nation. Chief Ingo," the Princess said, "What did you know of this?"

"Brakos paid me to give him a map of the coastline and the villages," he admitted, much chastened. "I didn't know what he intended. I thought the bandits were from Timur Laut and there was no connection with Brakos, honestly."

"You are either a traitor or a fool. We will continue your questioning later today, in a cell. In the meantime, I must speak with the Ambassador. We must stop this war before it starts. We have no quarrel with your people," She said, looking at the Ryzen.

"Nor we with yours," replied the Ambassador. "We are allies, with only peace between our people. This Brakos is the source of all the trouble, I truly believe. I have already sent messages to War Chief Cree and to the Grandmothers with my opinion. I have in my scrip a copy of the orders sent by the honored Cree telling me our nation's policy. Will you read it? It does not mention your people specifically, because the only threat we knew of was from Theralona, but the order applies to any peaceful nation." He reached into his scrip and handed a piece of parchment to the Princess.

Koakoula looked at it. "This is in your language. I cannot read it. Will you translate?"

The Ryzen did so, and the logic and reason of the orders calmed down most of the chiefs, who now turned their ire on Brakos and began demanding the Princess take action against him. It would be a long day, and a longer evening, until everyone had a say.

# # # # #

Guayota Cor

Three days after the emergency council of Princess Koukoula, a delegation from Theralona arrived in port. Assembly Delegate Androkes stepped off the boat with two assistants, who by their appearance also served as bodyguards. They were met by four members of the Princess' personal guard, who escorted them to the Hall.

Koakoula received them in the same place the emergency council had been held. The room was large for such a small delegation, but in Koakoulas' opinion it served to remind them that Guayota Cor was a significant city-state in Tenifra and, in fact, on the continent. Delegate Androkes introduced himself to the Princess and explained his purpose in making such a hurried journey.

"We sailed a night and half a day to reach you, Princess. You cannot imagine the chaos in Nesos City. The Assembly is divided; most wish to go to war with Timur Laut, but some of us believe this is a plot hatched by one of our own people out of his own ambition and greed. We have received messages relayed along our message chains by the swiftest birds. These messages told us that you were raided by bandits pretending to be from Timur Laut, but who were really Theralonians in disguise. I understand you have a prisoner in your holding rooms, one of these very bandits. Is it so?"

"It is, Delegate Androkes."

"Princess, I request extradition of this prisoner to Theralona. He has harmed your people, and you have a right to deal with him according to your laws. However, he may have information that must be brought before the Assembly before it embarks on a war that will cost thousands upon thousands more lives. May I take him to speak to our Assembly, and then return him to you for whatever punishment you deem fit?"

"You may, Delegate Androkes. The risk to all our countries should war break out again is certainly greater than the hurt we have suffered. Take him. If you put him to death, say that it is in payment for the lives of Tenifran villagers under the protection of Guayota Cor, as well as the wrong he has done to Theralona. This satisfies our honor as well as the need to stop a war. Are we in agreement?"

"This I can promise; if justice is done and his actions are condemned, I will remember your people when he pays the

price. If the Assembly is too foolish to listen, however, I may have no further recourse. Should the fools continue to believe this Brakos and rush blindly into war, he may die for telling your people about Brakos' plans. With this understanding, I agree to your terms."

"Done. We will bring him here to you after you have refreshed yourselves and had food and drink. Will your oarsmen wish to come ashore?"

"No, they will rest in shifts. I will stay to break bread with you, but we must start back immediately. The Assembly meets the day after tomorrow. I have barely enough time to make the return journey with the prisoner."

"I understand. Let it be so."

#   #   #   #   #

The prisoner, who said his name was Degos, was unhappy. He insisted he didn't want to go back to Theralona because he was afraid of Brakos.

"He'll kill me, yes he will, honored sir," he whimpered as he sat on a bench on the deck of the Delegate's boat. His ankles were chained to the bench to avoid escape attempts; he had tried twice to jump overboard already. He was clearly terrified.

"Why are you so afraid? Isn't he your leader?" Androkes asked.

"He were, sir. That he were. I didn't know he wanted to paint me and put a wig on me and tell me to kill children, no I didn't, sir. That ain't right, no it isn't."

"He ordered you to kill children?"

"He said to kill everyone in the house. They's children in the house, so that means to kill children. That ain't right."

"Did you actually kill children, then?"

"Course I did. Brakos would get angry if I didn't. But I don't like it, no I don't. It ain't right. He made me do it."

"You'll pay for that when we reach Theralona, but first you have to speak to the Assembly and tell them all about Brakos making you do these things. What did he tell you to say to the people you attacked?"

"We was to shout that we was doing this for the Ryzen and for the Grandmothers, whoever they is. Don't make sense to me. Killing children and blaming it on they grandmothers. That ain't right."

"But you did it anyway?"

"Brakos is mean. He hurts people."

The Delegate shook his head. "How does he hurt people, Degos? Do you know this, or is this just a story they tell?"

"Everyone knows Brakos hurts people. I seen one man with burn marks on the back of his legs. They said Brakos did that because he got mad at him."

"But you didn't see Brakos do that, did you?"

"No, I seen him yell at people, though. He yells a lot."

"You believe he would hurt you if he got mad at you?"

"Course he would. Everybody knows that."

"Do you think I would hurt you?"

Degos thought about it.

"No, sir, I doesn't think you would. You might kill me, but not on account of being mad, just if it were the law like. But you wouldn't hurt me just to be mean, and you wouldn't like it."

"And Brakos likes hurting people? How do you know this?"

"Everybody knows it. He's mean."

The Delegate sighed. There wouldn't be much sense gotten out of this one. Still, it was enough to present a strong case before the Assembly. He continued to question Degos as they journeyed; he slept in short spells, woke to see how much time they were making, and questioned the prisoner again. It was clear that the man knew he had been well paid; he gave the money to his woman before he left Nesos City, because she was carrying a child and had need to pay a midwife. He didn't appear to understand much, but dimly grasped that he was supposed to provide for it. He said he got on the boat with the others, and told Brakos he didn't mind doing a little killing. It paid better, you see. Ten drachs more that the oarsman job. Ten drachs was house rent for a year! Of course he said he'd do it. He wasn't stupid, no matter what everyone said.

Degos confirmed that Brakos ordered all of them to put a paste on their arms, legs, and face that made the skin look brown, and gave each of the landing party a black wig. The oarsmen just covered their hair with kerchiefs. He didn't know why they did this; rich people did strange things, and Brakos must be rich.

"Stands to reason, don't it. He can pay out all those drachs for what he wants done, he must be rich, and so he does strange things."

Androkes agreed that he did strange things.

They reached Nesos City at moonrise on the second day. The Assembly was set to meet the next morning. Androkes went gratefully to his house to get a few hours of much-needed rest; the guards took Degos to the Assembly holding rooms, where he was given a private room with two guards stationed outside the chamber.

\#   \#   \#   \#   \#

At first light, Androkes and his guards made their way to the Pavilion; their destination was the holding rooms underneath the Assembly Hall. Degos would be the first to speak before the Assembly today.

As he walked down the hallway, he heard a disturbance ahead. People were shouting and pounding on doors. He got close to Degos' chamber and saw the two guards. One was shaking his head; the other was looking sweaty and sick. Prisoners pounded on the locked doors, but the door to Degos' room was wide open. The warden of the holding rooms stood in the doorway, staring at whatever was inside.

Androkes joined the warden and looked into the room. He stared, frozen, gazing at the unexpected sight.

Degos hung by the neck on a rope tied to a beam across the ceiling. His hands were bound, and there was no stool or bench beneath his feet; nothing in the room that he could have used. His neck was a mass of bruises, and his face looked like he'd been in a bar fight.

"Killed himself, I reckon," said the warden. "It happens."

"Are you crazy? Look at him! His hands are tied. Look at those bruises, and the angle of his neck. It was broken, but not by the rope. Degos didn't kill himself."

"Sure he did," said the warden. "Brakos said so."

"Brakos? Is he here?"

"Left a message," the warden answered, pointing to the body hanging on the rope.

"What about the guards?"

"Had too much to drink and passed out. They'll get their pay docked for it, but some unknown benefactor will likely replace it. That's how it's done. Best not to question."

Sick at heart, Androkes and his guards went to the Assembly Hall, where the session had already begun. Senator Brakos himself was there, speaking to the Assembly.

"Noble sirs, hear me! We are under attack. The whole world is under attack, and it's due to those evil wizards of Timur Laut! My loyal men went to speak with their ambassador last week. He's a Ryzen, one of the wizards who fly in the sky and shoot magic from their staffs. My men fought bravely, but who can fight a wizard? With the touch of the magic staff, one became so sick he nearly died; one lost his sight for hours. The others were swept off their feet by magic and struck senseless. This is evil magic, noble sirs!

"Just two days ago the evil ones attacked a village in Tenifra and killed many people. Old men, women, children. They killed them while they slept. The peaceful people of Tenifra are our allies. They look to us for help. We must retaliate! I ask you to declare war on Timur Laut!"

The outcry in the room left no doubt of the outcome. One person after another told stories of the 'evil wizards', each story more fanciful than the last.

Androkes tried to argue for reason and was shouted down.

"Prove it! Bring your evidence!"

Of course, he had none. He had counted on Degos' testimony. Without it, there was only his opinion. In less than an hour, the Assembly voted and the Senate agreed. Theralona declared war on Timur Laut and gave Brakos the title of Commander of the armies and Ruler of the Seas. With his fleet of boats and Theralonias Navy it would be the biggest armada assembled in over 2 generations.

Chapter 12

"Once you truly know the Way broadly, you will see it in everything."

~CreeVa Kau, War Chief of the Nine Tribes, Senior Commander of the Ryzen

Tambak Citadel, Timur Laut

"Move it, Mouse! You're late!"

Maz laughed as he caught up with Lupo at their Sikka. The last week had been a stressful round of intense flyer training and strategic planning sessions with Uncle Cree, who he tried to think of as "War Chief." It wasn't that he didn't respect him; he was just so used to thinking of him as his uncle that any other role didn't seem natural. He was glad Uncle Cree was in charge of planning the war strategy, because there was no one better in all the lands.

"Yes sir! I'm moving it as fast as I can!"

Lupo growled, just to make a point even though he knew he wasn't late. "This Sikka isn't going to fly itself, you know. And you have a lot more to learn, One of these days you'll be a real pilot, and it better be soon. We have a planning meeting. There's new information."

Maz hurled himself into the pilot's seat, Lupo took the navigator station, and Jebel was already in his place at the techno station. As soon as all three Ichaks clicked into their sockets, Maz lifted the Sikka straight up in the air. He slid it forward a few paces horizontally, then went 90 degrees to vertical orientation. Inside the gravity repulsion bubble you don't feel the change in orientation which takes a few times to get used to. With no further warning, Maz zoomed straight out of the landing area and over to the Serpent Mound, where the War Chief had been having his briefings to be within easy reach of the Grandmothers. He hovered, returned to horizontal, and descended perfectly on to his assigned parking space. He cut power and twirled in his seat, hands in the air.

"Perfect landing! Again!"

"Yeah, alright. Not bad, could have been smoother. Now wipe that grin off your face and look like a Ryzen. I don't want the War Chief taking me to task for not teaching you proper decorum." Maz could tell Lupo was really pleased with how well he handled the Sikka, because otherwise he would have said he should go back and learn to walk since he obviously wasn't ready to fly.

"Thanks, boss. Are we meeting in the same place as last time?"

"And why not? It worked."

"Where do you want me, sir?" Jebel asked. "Should I wait with the Sikka?" One person had to remain with the vehicle under the current rules, and since the War Chief wanted Maz brought up to speed quickly, he had to attend all the meetings.

"That will work. We'll be back after the meeting. Make sure we are fuled and loaded and ready to go. Try not to fall asleep," Lupo said as he waved and walked off, Maz in tow. Jebel grinned and got to work.

It was only a short walk from the landing pad halfway up the hill to the meeting room in a side wing of the Grandmothers' Hall. Maz made sure his short unbleached vest was straight and had no obvious wrinkles. He admired the way Lupo's vest always looked as if it just emerged from the clothes press. He was getting used to Ryzen attire, the semi-formal uniform he wore now, primarily, as well as the formal set, which he had not yet worn, and the gray battle uniform, which he had worn once in a drill. It was different from a student tunic, but in a good way. It was armored, to be sure, but that wasn't its only purpose. It helped identify him to others, and reminded him who he was whenever he was at risk of forgetting. From time to time he slipped back into old habits, but just a glimpse of the uniform reminded him he was a Ryzen now, and there was no such thing as second best. He had to give everything, all the time. No exception.

Uncle Cree started with a brief meditation to focus the mind and thank the Creator, and started right into the substance of the meeting.

"We have been at war for some time, but now we have an official declaration, which should arrive by boat in a day. Good thing we have our information sources, since it looks like their first attack will probably arrive ahead of their declaration of war. They apparently wanted the element of surprise.

"Brakos, as we expected, is Commander of the Armies and Ruler of the Seas, in their language. According to our sources, he has been spending drachs like seawater. For those of you who have never been to Theralonia, those are the round metal discs they use for currency instead of beaded cloth strips the nine tribes of Timur Laut use as a means of exchange. He is hiring boat crews, fighting men, and something called "special officers" who are paid three times the regular pay. No one knows what their job is. Let's review what we know.

"In addition to hundreds, even thousands, of men and ships, they have something else."

"Women, I assume," said a female pilot. There was laughter, quickly stifled.

"Don't assume, pilot. You'll be wrong. They have no women in battle positions. In fact, except in some outlying villages, women of Nesos have no work other than housekeeping." He smiled at their astonished expressions. "Know your enemy. It is the only way to defeat them."

"Now, what I've learned is that in addition to harnessing the energy we call silverwater, which is from the old knowledge both our people share, they have a weapon they call "fire of the gods". I don't know for sure what it is, but it isn't a symbolic name for zeal or enthusiasm. It's an actual weapon, probably having something to do with … guess what? Fire. Also, they have three functioning Sikka Manu."

This brought a rumbling of displeasure.

"Yes, it is our sworn duty to recover and protect the ancient gifts. We are going to recover them and he will bring them to us. We know they can't access anything other than basic operation from the Sikka Manu, so Brakos won't have knowledge of what they can fully do. We know they will have managed to get the Sikka in the air and fly in basic training mode. We know the arrogance of Brakos will mean he will most likely be flying one of the Sikka himself. That's not going to affect our strategy. He is most likely attempting to try to set a trap. That has been his method so far. We will use that. Here's what we're going to do… "

#   #   #   #   #

Maz carefully hovered his Sikka in the designated spot. He was high enough to avoid detection from the ground. When the sun set, his flyer would be invisible from below, with its dark painted surface. He was nervous, of course; this was the real thing, not a training exercise. Real people would kill other real people in a war. And the war wasn't over the usual things; borders, resources, injustices. It was to enrich one man and put him in positions of power. The enemy was as much of a victim as his own people were. This couldn't be allowed to go forward. He had to be a part of stopping it.

"Sir," he asked Lupo, "How is it that Brakos is able to operate a Sikka? I thought they required at least one Ryzen. Does he have a captured Ryzen, do you think?"

"That's possible," said Lupo, "But there's a more likely scenario. You know Brakos studied at the Academy many years ago? Well, in his day just as in yours, basic flight theory was a required subject. Brakos possibly would have been around and seen enough to get a Sikka in the air and bring it down safely, even if he was never trained. He will not be a skilled flyer and he doesn't know the true capabilities the Sikka have. I don't think a captured Ryzen could be forced against his will; his Ichak wouldn't cooperate, even with threats to his life. Brakos can't possibly know about the link we have with our Ichaki. We know he probably has at least one Ichak, four are missing. One of the captured flyers had two Ryzen in its crew, and therefore would have had two Ichaki on site. We found one of their bodies, Kal the crew chief on your brother's Sikka but none the others yet, sadly we assume they met the same fate. He probably wondered why he couldn't power up the Sikka Manu, and my suspicion is that he finally figured it out and put the Ichaki in the sockets. Odds are he's flying one himself and picked out a couple of minions to fly the other two. He could have trained them. They don't have to do a lot of maneuvering."

"What do you mean, they don't have to maneuver? How can they fight?"

"The villages we're protecting won't have Sikka Manu to defend them. At least, Brakos won't think they do. He thinks he's attacking undefended villages who aren't expecting an air attack. He'll have his boats and his land troops, too. They can do a lot of damage. But imagine the effect on a simple village if they saw three Sikka Manu fighting for the other side! The consequences would be devastating. And as you know from your studies, emotional warfare is a huge part of any military effort." we don't want the villagers to think the Ryzen attacked them.

"He can power up a Sikka if the Ryzen whose staff he's using is dead?"

"Probably. If he learned the sequence, he can do a partial power up, to put it in maintenance mode. Adding an Ichak and the Capaicha would make the Sikka react as it would with a Ryzen flying with a student as a training officer. It will think the pilot is a student, and it's normal to use the training Ryzens weapon and helmet to activate the Sikka. Not that they think, of course. They operate at a subconscious level. But it's enough to get the machine in the air on a "training flight" without confusing the Sikka and causing it to shut down. Don't worry, we have the advantage in the air and Brakos has no idea what a fully operational Sikka with a skilled pilot is capable of.``

\# \# \# \# \#

Maz had a lot to think about as they stood guard over their designated section of the coastline. He might be meeting Sikka

Manu in battle, not just ground troops. Going over in his mind the theories of air battle he'd been taught, he tried to imagine what that would be like in this very place. Perhaps a shadow would appear right over there in the sea, a fleet of boats … and then a darkness might appear in the sky above it … he could almost see it.

"There! Do you have anything yet?"

Maz shook his head. "What? Where?"

"Focus! Calm your thoughts so you can listen to the Sikka. I've activated search mode. We will be able to sense when any one of them is in range; it's just like talking to other crews, except they can't hear us. Remember our orders. As soon as we locate one, we call it in to the other crews and they will head to us to assist." Lupo seemed very confident. Maz was nervous but was doing his best not to show it.

"Wait, I'm getting something, almost like a dream... I think one, yes, one sikka is coming, from the east right about where the sun will rise," Maz said with a bit more excitement.

"Make the call, Jebel. Let everyone know this is where the fun will happen," Lupo said in the same relaxed calm voice he used to order food at the falu pau.

"I think I can see them now, boats on the ocean. And a shadow in the sky above. Hard to see in the dark, but they're there if you focus."

Maz hadn't been imagining it. They were right where he'd thought something might appear; he needed to learn to trust his instincts.

"I see them. So we wait."

It was incredibly difficult to follow the orders he'd been given, to wait until they reached the shore or until they appeared to have seen them. In the growing dusk, not quite full dark, remaining motionless held their best promise of remaining undetected. The Sikka could hover over a spot without appearing to move, maintaining position over the earth through its gravity repulsion alone. Unlike a bird which had to keep moving to remain aloft, the downward repulsion balanced with the same amount of attraction—the same principle that operated in their Ichak—kept them hovering in one place, not calling attention to their presence. But waiting was so hard! Maz wanted to be doing something. It was true, the thing they taught him; the most dangerous enemy was himself. His own impulses, his weakness, could undo everything if he failed to master them. Master yourself, then master your opponent, Cree said during staff training. Phrases his uncle used came back to him over and over as he hovered in the air before his first battle. Be in the moment, not in last night's dinner; that used to make no sense, but now all he could think about was the meal he had enjoyed hours ago, and the last meal he had with his father, and the last glimpse of his sister on the training field as she walked to her own vehicle. Purposely, he refocused and waited.

The boats anchored just outside the surf line. The shore was still; there was no sign of the people Maz knew were waiting at the edge of the village. No sign of the waiting Ryzen on the ground standing with the villagers; no sign of the Sikka Manu hovering above. Below his position, he saw the movement of a Sikka just above the landing party wading from the boats to the shore. Still, he waited. And waited.

Lupo gripped his staff as it rested in its socket. When the command was given, he heard it—or felt it—through the Ichak. He took a breath.

"Now!"

Maz moved, shifting the Sikka to vertical as he adjusted his position, then back to horizontal as he descended. His objective was to hover directly over the attacking forces, so Jebel and Lupo could use their Ichak to hold them in place. The first target was the Sikka Manu. If they could recover it at the start, it would stop the battle right at its beginning, and if they could catch Brakos before he slithered away they could cut the head off the snake before it struck. As he approached, however, the boats began to open fire on the town with a large ballista mounted to the decks, one of the flaming projectiles whizzed between the two sikka and impacted the trees behind the town. By now the Sikka below him detected his presence, and it reversed direction and sped away, at training speed. They could easily catch it, but that would mean leaving the village unprotected. The ships and the troops attacking from below on the beach needed to be dealt with first.

Clearly, the pilot of the Sikka had his own plan, heading for safety instead of providing cover for his land troops. The boats, seeing the fleeing Sikka, also reversed direction, clearly following orders, but of course they were not as fast.

Maz had his orders, too. Capture as many as possible. His orders conflicted with his desire to pursue the Sikka Manu, but the orders were clear. Take prisoners from the landing party to get information out of them; recapture the Sikka Manu; stop remaining forces by any means possible. Orders were orders.

He maneuvered over the landing party, who were now running for the waves and their retreating boats. They were clearly untrained troops, skilled at murdering sleeping villagers but not ready to face the armed men who now ran towards them or the vehicles that hovered overhead. Bandits from the docks and alleys of Nesos City, not professional troops. Brakos had to work with what he had, but these weren't all he had.

This was a raid, perhaps a trial of the Sikka Manu. Maz noted they flew it in horizontal position, as Uncle Cree had predicted, rather than going vertical for maximum speed and maneuverability. Maybe he didn't know about the vertical position. The motion of the craft was sluggish, not as responsive as his own; again, the War Chief was right. There were no Ryzen aboard those Sikka Manu, just the stolen Ichak from the murdered Ryzen on the supply runs. The staffs of the dead, with no partnered minds to guide them, were nothing but power sources. They wouldn't be usable as weapons, either.

The Sikka Manu in the hands of Brakos and his crew were transportation only, not weapons in their own right.

It took little time to sink the small group of 20 ships. Lupo, who usually never showed emotion in combat, had a huge smile on his face from getting to use the Sikkas' pipes in a real battle for his first time ever. It was like target practice for him, as he blew holes through the hulls of the ships. Most of the enemy sailors were able to swim back to the beach or find floating debris to hang on to until they were picked up; the soldiers that landed on the beach to attack quickly saw what was happening to the fleet and laid down their weapons. They were captured and taken for questioning, where Maz had no doubt they would easily be persuaded to give up information in exchange for their lives and an eventual hope of returning to their own country, to await whatever punishment might be given by the authorities once the extent of Brakos' plotting was known. For now, they were valuable for the information in their heads.

The next battle would see the ferocity that had marked the armies of Timur Laut in the Great War thirty years ago. They would be ready to meet the enemy.

Chapter 13

"In battle, if you make your opponent flinch, you have already won."

~CreeVa Kau, War Chief of the Nine Tribes, Senior Commander of the Ryzen

Tambak Citadel, Timur Laut

A state of alert preparation filled the city. It was like the feeling before a race or sporting contest, thought Maz, but a dozen dozen times more intense. It reminded him of the energy in the barn back at Uncle Cree's farm right before the grappling matches started, multiplied again and again. People were running or walking swiftly, everyone with something important to do. War Chief Cree had issued a decree that for the safety of all citizens they should take shelter or leave the Tambak citadel for the next two days. People were bustling about making their preparations. The defense force was bringing in carts of dirt to use for putting out fires and fortifying the defence from beach landings. The massive stone blocks that made up the citadel, most weighing more than four mammoths and some nearly 20, could withstand anything Theralonia and Brakos could throw at them, but the fire could devastate property and life.

Maz had returned to the city just a few hours ago, had a short nap, a brief visit with his parents, and was now on his way to a strategy session at the flying field. He knew the plan in general terms, of course; the War Chief had issued general orders as soon as the first round of interrogations ended. The Ryzen didn't need to be reminded of the orders; they all understood the intent with every fiber of their being. Engage the enemy, capture the Sikka Manu intact, preserve the ancient technology at all costs. But there must be no extra effort to take prisoners alive; the time for taking prisoners had passed.

Brakos was not only a politician; he was a profiteer. He promised wealth to his soldiers from unlimited looting, sold the rights to captured technology to businessmen in Nesos, and kept a percentage of everything for himself. His plan had been in the works for years, while he had a small fleet of ships for his unsanctioned raids. He had been using those boats for piracy while he put the rest of his plan in place. He now had almost 400 ships at his disposal. He bought politicians, and bribed or blackmailed as many Delegates as he could. Maz could hardly imagine the complexity of the plan. His mind didn't work that way. He had heard some of the details from Lupo when they talked between workouts and tasks.

Lupo soon would be at the flying field. Maz realized he had better get there before him and complete all his checks before taking their Sikka up to the charging station on the Mound. By the time Lupo got there at sunrise they would be ready to go to the meeting, which was being held at a hidden landing field further south to avoid listening ears. One of the things the captured enemy disclosed was that spies were already placed in the capital, and in spite of enthusiastic questioning it appeared they really didn't know who they were, just that Brakos got information from them. Supposedly, there were spies in the Hall of the Ryzen, probably service employees who would not be noticed. An offsite meeting would provide more security than the normal meeting rooms.

One of the things the questioners found out was the nature of "fire of the gods". It was a weapon; somehow it would be thrown or dropped, and the impact would cause it to catch fire. Lupo thought there must be two substances that burst into flame when combined, and perhaps the devices containing them had a separation that would break on impact. This would be a good weapon to research and find a way to stop its future use. The exact nature of the weapon's construction was unknown to Lupo but he was sure War Chief Cree had encountered it before in the Great War. He made a mental note to ask about it later when Cree wasn't so busy. The prisoners were certain it existed, having seen a demonstration back in Nesos. The frightening thing about this "fire of the gods" was that it could not be quenched with water. It had to be smothered, completely deprived of air, in order to be put out. That made it useful as a naval weapon. Fire was always a risk on board a ship, but water was plentiful to put it out, though not an easy task. A type of fire that water could not touch? It could be very dangerous. Maz shuddered. It didn't bear thinking about.

As he neared the heart of the city, he realized that growing up here his whole life he had always taken for granted the beauty of the architecture and the incredible engineering it took to build such grand megalithic structures. The entire city was laid out as a mirror image of the heavens above. Running down the center of town was a canal, or more correctly, a series of giant reflecting ponds that ran the same angle as the Path of the Dead in the sky, with its cloudy river of countless stars. The temples, buildings, and shops were all laid out in accordance with the major celestial objects in the sky, the sun,the moon, and the constellations. Maz fondly remembered his father taking him and his brother for walks all through the city when they were just little boys, teaching them about the stars and their positions in the sky and the legends and stories of how they got there. He realized more than ever that protecting this place, his home, was of great importance; it gave him a sense of pride that he was in a position to do just that. He hurried his pace, more determined than ever to be the best Ryzen he could be.

Maz planned on being early for the meeting so he would have all the maintenance on the Sikka done before Lupo and Jebel got there, not to impress them, but to make sure he and his crew would be ready to be the best they could, and to make sure they would be in the fight first. He was almost finished when Lupo and Jebel arrived, both holding a carafe of hot kafi and giving him a silent smile and nod of approval. "Let's get to the briefing, Mouse," said Lupo.

War Chief Cree stood to the side of the hanger as he gave Squadron Chief Matay the duty of giving the briefing to the Ryzen.

"Here is what we know as of this morning. Brakos' fleet is heading our way with almost 400 ships. They will be off our shores before midday. The stolen Sikka have not been located, which means either he is holding them back or he has them powered down because he knows we can detect them. Brakos will definitely bring them to the fight; he can't afford not to. The question is, when will he show them? Our plan will be to leave one Sikka at the Citadel and position half the Sikka Manu to the north and the other half to the south. This should prevent him from trying to flank us and to be the hammers when the trap is sprung. Remember, the weapons on board his fleet are formidable. Don't underestimate them; a well-placed shot could put you out of flight mode and you will be going for a swim. When you engage, remember not to turn your belly forward to any ship. The best tactic will be to position yourselves as directly above them as possible. They cannot aim the ballista straight up. Now, who would like to volunteer to be the bait in the middle?"

Without hesitation, every Ryzen hand went up. That put a big smile on Matay's face.

"Good," he said. "Then, whose Sikka is ready to leave immediately?"

Lupo, Maz, and Jebel all kept their hands up.

"Excellent! Darkwolf will take position over the citadel, the crew of the Dancing Bear and I will remain concealed in the Citadel to back you up. Sun Squadron to the south and Moon Squadron to the north, move out!"

Lupo turned to Maz with a look of amazement. He clearly hadn't expected him to be so quick to volunteer. "You know, I'm really starting to like you, Mouse."

As they all were leaving the briefing and heading to the hangar, Dom caught up to Maz and put his arm around him. "Ahh, you lucky dog, I wish I had your spot. Be strong out there and be safe!"

"You as well, brother. I'll see you after," Maz replied; they bumped fists and headed off to battle.

Walking to the hangar, Maz noticed this was the first time he had seen all the Ryzen together in full battle dress. He was beyond proud he was in his gray battle uniform, as were his crewmates; The vests of the gray battle uniforms were originally designed by the first Ryzen, long ago. All of them looked the same, presumably to avoid having leaders stand out and become prime targets. Narrow piping on the tunic collar identified the rank, but all the uniforms were otherwise the same; gray tunic, gray trousers, long gray battle vest secured with a belt. The vests were constructed of small lightweight metal overlapping plates intricately woven together that gave an appearance up close similar to fish scales. They were extremely good at deflecting weapons and projectiles; they were lightweight and allowed freedom of movement. The battle vests were all very old, from the old learning. The belts held hand weapons like knives and teki, the iron claws that fastened over the knuckles. Ground troops other than Ryzen carried bows and arrows and scimitars, but Ryzen had enough with their Ichaki.

Taking his place inside Darkwolf, and putting on his capaicha, then grasping his Ichak, Maz carefully piloted the craft out of the hanger, careful not to make the slightest mistake, not just because it would hurt the craft, but because every other crew was watching them leave first. He would never hear the end of it if he even barely bumped anything. Ryzen were relentless at making fun of each other for mistakes. He laughed to himself that he was almost more worried about that than going into battle.

"Hold position here." Lupo gave the order.

"Hurry up and wait," Jebel said, getting comfortable in his seat. "Keep scanning for those Sikka, Maz; that fleet will be here soon, and we are a big shiny target."

"I'm on it," said Maz.

Time moves slowly when you are in a heightened sense of alert.

What seemed like half a day was in reality barely enough time to sit down for the evening meal. Slowly bringing the view into focus by squinting his eyes hard, Maz was able to begin to make out the barely visible outline of a fleet of ships on the horizon.

"I think I see something!" shouted Maz with a little higher pitch in his voice than normal, as Lupo noticed.

"Relax, Mouse. It will take them a while to get here. Any sense of the stolen Sikka Manu out there?"

"Negative, I'm only sensing Squadron Chief Matay and his Sikka behind us," Maz replied.

"Alright then, you know the orders; until Brakos shows himself we will hold this position and let them come to us. We have the greater range with our weapons. I will keep them from getting too close; Jebel, be ready with the interceptor. Once we are in battle, I will begin informing the squadron," Lupo said, shifting his controls over to the Sikka's main weapon, the wailu kile pipe.

Matay overheard the voices from the Darkwolf and began to speak with them directly through the Sikka's communication utility.

"Crew Chief Lupo, This is Squadron Chief Matay. Dancing Bear is in position; as soon as we identify the stolen Sikka we will engage and take them down and then go clean up th…"

BOOM!... BOOM!... BOOM!....

Tahari was standing out in front of one of the last open falu paus that had not closed, even though the War Chief had recommended that for safety all people should leave. The owner of this falu pau was an old man who had served on the defense force in the great war and he was not about to be scared off by some rogue Theralonian, he eagerly informed Tahari while preparing her order. She was going to bring one of her father's favorite dishes, spicy aurochs with tomatoes wrapped in cornbread, to him and her mother while they were taking shelter in his research lab until it was safe.

BOOM!! BOOM!! BOOM!! Three explosions, in rapid sequence.

Then the screams started. She turned, and saw flames on the roof of a shop across the street. The flames were spreading incredibly quickly. She ran into the street, and saw a Sikka far overhead, dropping what looked like clay pots from the cabin down on the city. The pots broke on impact, exploded, and just as the prisoners described, immediately burst into flame. At that moment she realized they were under attack from the gates to the east of the city, clay pots and arrows coming from over the wall by who knows how many invaders. She must get to her mother and father right away, she thought. She turned to run, forgetting about the food she had ordered.

Then she noticed people were running with buckets of water. Tahari remembered what she had heard from Maz.

"No water! Orders of the Ryzen! Use the dirt from the carts! Smother the fire! Water makes it spread! No water!" she shouted it over and over, and others took up the cry. But dirt was harder to haul in a bucket than water, and the fires kept spreading. People ran to get valuables and family members out of their homes and shops. In just moments, everything was chaos.

Tahari ran as fast as she could towards the lab, thankful that the roofs of most of the city weren't thatch, as too many roofs in the market were. Thatch would have gone up in flames at the first touch of fire. The laboratory in the tower was safe, too, as it was under a thick stone roof. That had been the rule since ancient times, and Tahari wondered if the ancients must have been familiar with this "fire of the gods". The Theralonians' ancestors must have used it in the Great War, and in wars before that. It was truly a horrible weapon. Where the fire touched human flesh, it began to burn even more furiously, as if the flesh and blood added power to the flame. The screams of the wounded were the most terrible thing she had ever heard.

Lungs bursting, she arrived at her father's office. She saw fires on the ground, but the defense forces were beating the flames with blankets and smothering them as soon as they started. Some were throwing handfuls of dirt mixed with an anti-fire substance that was kept in barrels that they had brought in, another practice from old times.

"Tahari!" cried Tamu. "Hurry!"

Putting on a burst of speed, she arrived at the door to the science building, and Tamu grabbed her by the hand to drag her in, shutting the door behind her.

"Downstairs! The lower levels here will be safe. There are tunnels that run outside the walls. We will be safe down there, and we can escape if they breach the gates. Your mother has water for us, and probably something to eat."

Tahari managed a weak smile, in spite of her terror. It was nice to know that her parents were the same as always, even though fire rained from the sky and the city was in flames around them. She followed her father into a conference room, where her mother ran and hugged her.

"We have to leave," Tahari said to them.

Bahi responded with a look of despair on her face. "Your father won't leave his research."

Tamu tried to reassure them both. "I will be fine, this building is solid stone built in the ancient ways. The flames cannot hurt me, but I must not let the fire burn my research. I have files stored up on the top level of this building. I have students carrying the records down here, but I must supervise.

"Tahari, you must take your mother to the healing center. There will be many injured defenders that will require a competent healer."

Tahari and Bahi reluctantly agreed to leave him, with the condition that Tamu come meet them at the healing center when it is safe. They left him the provisions bag Bahi had put together, and mother and daughter headed the normally short stroll over to the healing center at almost a full run.

When they got there it was organized chaos; the injured had already started coming in, mostly burns so far. Bahi rushed to get cleaned up to get to work and Tahari would stay with her to help in whatever way she could be of use.

Up above, the situation was unsettled. The bombs caught everyone by surprise. The crew at the flying field were in confusion for many moments. After a brief pause to listen for sounds, Lupo spoke through the communications embedded in his sikka.

"Matay, sir, are you alright?"

Matay responded in a very calm voice.

"We have taken a direct hit, but we are uninjured. We must land Dancing Bear, put out the flames, assess the damage and take care of the attackers at the gates. The stolen Sikka Manu are directly above. They must have been just out of sensing range until the moment they attacked. You have the lead, Crew Chief Lupo. You know the mission; go get our Sikka back."

Lupo,feeling a little nervous but trying not to show it, took action.

"Maz, get us up there now."

Maz engaged the gravity drive, turned the Sikka belly up and shot straight up faster than an arrow shot from a bow. By far his favorite part of piloting a Sikka was in gravity drive where you don't feel the motion or the pull of the earth anymore. He still marveled at the amazing craft every time he got to pilot one.

Once they were up in the air above the Citadel, he and his fellow Ryzen could see the situation at a glance. They were being attacked on three fronts. The three stolen Sikka Manu flew high above in circles over the city, dropping firebombs. But the immediate threat came from the army attacking the gates of the city, around 200 soldiers from the looks of it, pounding at the walls and gate with battering rams. Matay and his crew would have a lot of work to do. With the Ryzen distributed around the coastline handling small skirmishes that had clearly been set up to be a distraction, and only a third gone back to the city to assist, the outlook at the gates was grim. Catapults outside the walls flung clay jars of fire into the city, adding to the fires caused by the aerial bombardment.

Lupo grasped his Ichak and activated the communication portal of the capaicha. He spoke, more to focus his thoughts than because sound was needed, sending his message on an open frequency. Any Ryzen in the area would hear him.

"Ryzen Crew Chief Lupo here above the city, position 72. Squadron Chief Matay is grounded, I have point above, we have a visual on the stolen Sikka, we have ground forces attacking the city and the fleet is moving into range. We could use some assistance if any of you are not too busy."

A chorus of voices spoke into the minds of all three Ryzen. "Chief Lupo, this is Assistant Crew Chief Omah." "This is Assistant Crew Chief Maki." One by one they signed in, naming their positions. "Stalking Lion on our way to your position." "Screaming Monkey inbound." "Ryzen Gehn, Flying Serpent heading to you." "Ryzen Ybarra, Laughing Jackal on our way." Lupo realized he was the most senior among them. When the flow of names stopped, he went back on line.

"Ryzen, this is Crew Chief Lupo. I have command under Squadron Chief Matay's orders."

"Aye, sir, you have command," as one voice in their heads through their capaicha. Their ship was the command ship, however improbable that would have seemed just moments ago, at least until someone more senior arrived at the battle.

Senior Chief Matay had assumed command of the ground battles once he had realized Brakos' strategy to attempt to overwhelm them with a three pronged attack. Maz, while most junior, was the main pilot of their crew because of his expertise in the Academy, and because Lupo was unusually skilled with weapons systems and was command trained. Jebel was excellent at navigation, comms and engineering, but not as good at piloting, which was fine with him; he wasn't as interested in piloting. The mix made for a perfect crew.

So here they were; Maz was lead pilot in a fleet of mostly new Ryzen. This was what they had all been training for, and it was time for the ultimate test.

Lupo quickly outlined the strategy. He assigned a position along a circle around the city to each Sikka. The objectives were simple; to capture the enemy Sikka Manu, use the full destructive Ryzen capability to destroy the incoming fleet until they turned back, and assist the ground battle from above, as quickly as possible. Lupo assigned the other Sikka to fly position 360, around the stolen Sikka .

Maz went vertical and flew quickly to intercept. As he got close, all three Sikka began to dive. Maz immediately gave chase and matched the descent, then increased his speed, slowly gaining on the fleeing sikka. But which one was Brakos in? He had to concentrate and listen to the sounds coming from inside all three Sikka Manu. He just had to sort out all the various sounds and senses and find him.

Maz could actually hear what was going on in the cabins of the other Sikka without them trying to communicate with him. His Ichak was Truthseeker, and it had another attribute beyond telling lies; it could find information if Maz focused properly. Something... where was it? That one! There,on the left.

"Point 5 by 4, lock on, Jebel!" Maz realized he was barking orders to a higher rank Ryzen, but there was no time for formalities in the heat of battle.

When Matay and his crew got there, he realized it was an area of extremely heavy fighting. Ground forces were concentrated there, defending the gates, but they were almost overwhelmed. Brakos must have snuck a huge force up the shoreline to the north and back around behind the capital, then set up the southern raid as a distraction, he thought. Was that why he had turned and fled as soon as he saw Sikka Manu? Perhaps he was afraid, but more likely he fled to get back and lead the major force against the city. The bombers from the stolen Sikka threw the jars at what seemed to be carefully selected targets, such as major civic buildings and important residences. The residential area that housed many Professors and Guildmasters, was under heavy attack, with fires springing up on rooftops and in the streets. Further in, the Academy and the University were also on fire, suffering heavy ground attack. Brakos had chosen to personally target people in their homes; it wouldn't be safe to stay here.

Matay, Dalini, and Sidu headed to the western gate. The crash of the battering ram was deafening. It wouldn't be long before they would break through the iron reinforced wooden doors.

"So are we just going to jump in the middle?" Dalini asked matter of factly.

Matay glanced back at him. "Yes."

"And you know we will be surrounded then?" Sidu chimed in.

"Yes," responded Matay. " Then we will have them right where we want them."

"Time to have some fun!" Dalini said with a big smile on his face.

All three held their Ichaks parallel to the ground and engaged the repulsion power; they shot up in a smooth arc over the high wall and straight into the bulk of the opposing forces, landing with a shockwave that knocked enemy soldiers off their feet all around them. Three skilled Ichak-wielding Ryzen stood firm, surrounded by two hundred of Theralonia's best warriors. The

Ryzen, standing with their backs to each other, let the enemy come to them.

Wave after wave of enemy soldiers fell under the powerful swinging, thrusting, and crushing streams of power coming from the three Ichaks. In this triangle formation the Ryzen were able to control the number of enemies that could attack them at a time. Only three or four could approach each Ryzen, and if any slipped past the swinging and crushing arc of the Ichak, they would get blown back by the repulsion energy or touched by the secondary power at the end of the staff. Dozens of soldiers were either wandering around blindly, vomiting, or lying on the ground too weak to get up. Still more came at them, but now one of the Theralonian captains ordered them to only attack from one side. The advantage they had was less now.

"Time to get more aggressive," Matay said to his men; the communication through the capaicha augmented his voice so they could hear him over the din of battle. Matay held his Ichak parallel to the ground and engaged the repulsor, not in a high arc, but straight into the wall of warriors in front of him, driving at least a dozen flat onto their backs. Dalini and Sidu quickly backfilled Matay's position and attempted to reform the triangle defensive posture, where they could cover each other's sides. The battle had been raging for a while now, and despite the superb physical condition of Matay and his crew, their bodies would begin getting fatigued if they kept up this pace for much longer.

Just then, in the midst of all that commotion, a shockwave sent enemy soldiers flying in all directions just off their right flank. They looked to see who it was; it had to be another Ryzen.

As the Ryzen stood up they recognized the silver winged capaicha, brown fur lined coat and Bear Claw necklace of War Chief Cree.

Maz steered the Sikka to a position directly over Brakos, while Jebel grabbed the stolen vehicle with the sikka's attraction energy. Holding a delicate balance of the opposing energies, he kept the enemy vehicle in his grip while Maz flew away from the residential area.

Lupo called out to the other Ryzen Sikka Manu, "We are locked on one, the rest of you take down two and three."

Brakos was going crazy at the controls attempting to get away as they flew, unable to break free of the unseen grip, Brakos screamed at his crewman, ordering him to throw jars of fire at the Sikka that carried them like a raptor bird with a mouse in its claws. He gestured and shouted, and his meaning was clear, but it is not so easy to throw an object upwards from an open hatch at a moving target. One of the jars fell and broke on the captive Sikka, leaving nothing they could do to stop the growing flames. Brakos' crew retreated back into the cabin, not about to be burned by their own weapons.

Once Maz and Jebel had forced down the stolen Sikka to a low hovering level, Jebel locked them together in hover, facing hatch to hatch so they could board it. He would remain onboard to keep the ships locked together; Lupo and Maz Left their Ichaks behind, since there was not enough room to wield one properly inside the cabin of a Sikka anyway. Maz stepped out on the exterior of the ship, with Lupo at his back.

This was the moment Maz had been waiting for. He hadn't been certain it would happen, but ever since the day they heard of Draq's death, he had thought about what he would do when he was finally able to confront his brother's killer. As a Ryzen, Maz knew he shouldn't act out of anger and emotion. Cree always said that's when you make mistakes. Now, there was no time for mistakes. Maz had to put revenge out of his mind; he knew he must remain calm, no matter what. Seeking his intrinsic energy, he took a deep breath and cleared his thoughts, as he opened the hatch and jumped into the fray.

Just a few steps and he was at the hatch of the enemy craft. The inside of the cabin wouldn't be the ideal fighting arena, but the outside didn't offer secure footing. Although their boots contained flecks of wailu kile tuned to the attraction frequency, it was still possible to fall off the outside of a vehicle. This was not like fighting in a training ring.

Maz struck the emergency latch on the vehicle, opening the hatch. He was first through the hatch, with Lupo right behind him. Immediately, he was confronted by one of Brakos' men trying to lock his arm around Maz's neck; he spotted a knife in the other hand. Maz responded by instinct and training, braced his feet, and kept his posture straight; he reached behind his attacker's back, over the shoulder and grabbed his face under the chin, simultaneously grabbing and controlling the far arm to avoid getting stabbed. Stepping in with his leg behind his attacker's leg, Maz pulled him backwards over his leg and threw him straight down to the floor of the Sikka's cabin. He ripped the knife from his hand and added a few punches to the bridge of his nose to keep him from wanting to continue. In the midst of this, Lupo flew through the hatch and tackled the third crewman, who was about to jump on Maz. Lupo quickly had him pinned on the floor, battering his face with downward elbow strikes. The face of the crewman quickly turned red with blood, and he stopped resisting. Maz was up and turning just in time to see Brakos charging him.

Brakos, as Maz saw him for the first time, was as large as he had been described; that is, big, quite a bit larger than Maz. He was about a full hand-span taller, maybe more, and outweighed him by half a pig's weight. His light brown hair was cut short, Nesos style, and in loose curls half a finger length long all around his head; his blue eyes were furious. He crashed into Maz and drove him up against the bulkhead of the Sikka, throwing punches all the while. Maz leaned in, defensively blocking and catching the larger man's arms. Clearly Brakos had never encountered anyone trained in close-in fighting; he had expected Maz to pull away. Maz rolled Brakos to the ground, trying to trap him against the deck of the craft. Brakos twisted halfway down, spun around and lunged at Maz once again, using the same technique.

Not too bright, thought Maz. He's doing the same move over again. He's big, and he hasn't had to think about strategy. I can do this.

When the big man struck this time, Maz was ready. He sprawled his legs out and moved his hips forward. Keeping pressure on Brakos' back, Maz quickly spun around and positioned himself behind him, where he slipped his arm under the chin and pulled him backwards. In that moment, Maz remembered this was the same move Dom had done to him all those months ago back on the farm. Locking his legs around Brakos' torso, he began to tighten up the choke and put more pressure on the sides of the neck, by sliding his hand behind Brakos' head and pushing it forward as Cree had taught him. This was the moment Maz had been thinking about in his dreams; he tightened a little more. Prison for Brakos is what the grandmothers would probably want, he knew, but he couldn't allow this poison to contaminate any others in the world. He had almost convinced himself he was making a cold and rational decision that he must stop Brakos now. He told himself he wasn't thinking about Draq at all. Not at all. He tightened the choke a bit more.

Just then he felt a searing pain in his calf muscle. He realized he must have been stabbed, as Brakos struck with a short blade he had hidden in his wide belt. Maz growled in pain, still maintaining his choke hold. He squeezed tighter.

Lupo looked over and saw what was happening. He leapt off his bloodied opponent, then dove at Brakos and grabbed the wrist holding the blade, pulling it out of Maz's flesh and preventing him from twisting it around and doing more damage. Maz let go with his right hand, still with Brakos' throat in the crook of his left elbow, and Lupo placed the knife in his grasp.

Much to his surprise, the feeling of the knife in his hand was familiar. It felt like the knife in his belt, made by his brother Draq. Was it possible? Maz glanced down and realized it was indeed his brother's blade, the one that wasn't found with his body. He recognized the pattern of the metal as well as the maker's mark on the hilt. It was fitting. This man had killed his brother; not just ordered the kill, he had done it with his own hands or he would not have the knife. Now Maz had it. It had come home. He raised it, slipped it under his forearm to place it against the throbbing blood vessels in Brakos' neck, and whispered in his ear.

"Thanks for bringing my brother's knife home. Now it evens the score, Brakos. Draq was my brother. You killed him. Prepare to die," he said, as he slowly and calmly sliced open the side of Brakos' neck.

As they watched the life flow from Brakos, Lupo took off his belt and tied it around the top of Maz's calf to slow the blood flow.

"Let's go get you patched up, Ryzen", Lupo said.

Maz let go of Brakos, wiping the knife off on the bandit's tunic as he dropped him on the floor of the Sikka. Lupo lifted Maz up under his shoulder to bring him back into their Sikka, securing him in his seat as he called for the status of the other craft. "This is Acting Squadron Chief Lupo. Brakos is dead and

Sikka One is recovered. What is the status of Sikka Manu two and three?"

"Crew chef Ghen here. Number Three is recovered; they didn't put up much of a fight."

"Crew chief Oman here. Sikka Two recovered, same here. They didn't want any trouble."

"Good to hear. We have one injured Ryzen on the way to get patched up; the rest of you start taking apart that fleet. I will join you when I can," responded Lupo as he turned to Jebel.

"Jebel, bring our recovered Sikka back to the hanger, then find me at the healing tower landing pad."

Without a word, Jebel grabbed his Ichak and jumped into the burned and bloody recovered Sikka. Lupo slipped into the pilot's seat of Darkwolf for the short trip to the healers back at the Ryzen tower.

"So now it's Ryzen, not Mouse?" asked Maz, groggy from loss of blood and the post-battle adrenaline crash.

"You earned it."

The four elegantly and uniquely shaped Sikka Manu gleamed brightly in the midday sun with a bluish silver hue to the metal hulls. Known only to their crews and the other Ryzen as Stalking Lion, Flying Serpent, Screaming Monkey and Laughing Jackal, they headed towards the Theralonian fleet at blinding speed, and formed up in a diamond pattern directly above the attacking naval armada.

"This is crew chief Oman of the Stalking Lion. We are in position now; remember to stay out of range of the ballista. I don't want to have to go pick any of you up out of the water. Begin targeting the outer ships that could fire in our direction and work in. Fire when ready."

The well constructed oceangoing vessels of the Theralonain Navy were no match for the firepower and flight capabilities of the Ryzen Sikka Manu; they were simply fish in a barrel. Dom was beyond excited to be operating the Sikka's pipes on board the Flying Serpent. A Ryzen as new as himself would rarely have this opportunity to engage in battle. With no threats from the air and the superior position from directly above, the Ryzen had time to aim and take calm relaxed shots, one after another; before Dom knew it, he had surpassed Ryzen Lupo's numbers from the previous battle. The Theralonian fleet below was beginning to panic. Some of the ships were trying to flee, but were boxed in by others and began ramming each other to have room to maneuver. Some of the sailors decided they would rather take their chances swimming in the open water than be sitting ducks. Soon, obviously realizing the terrible position they were in a sizable group of ships, nearly a third of the fleet had managed to turn around and head back towards Theralonia. The Ryzen allowed them to do so. The rest of the fleet would soon be at the bottom of the ocean. Then they would send out their own ships to pick up any survivors.

Matay and his crew were busy with enemies in front of them, but they couldn't help but to try to get a glance at the War Chief in battle. Cree was as fast and strong as, if not stronger and faster, than Ryzen half his age; his technique was flawless, and the enemy soldiers were flying upside down through the air all around him. His Ichak seemed to sing as he effortlessly wielded it like it was no heavier than a feather. Dozens of bodies were stacking up around him. Matay and his crew were in awe. They began to fight their way towards the War Chief to link up with him. At that moment, they heard the unmistakable sound of a Sikka above them. Matay noticed the eyes of the Theralonians looking up at it; he spun around with a swing of his staff to get a look, and recognized it as one of the stolen ones. Was it Brakos? Were they losing the battle?

Jebel maneuvered the Sikka over to the west gate and saw the fighting going on; he saw the flash of Ryzen Ichaks. Those that were left of Brakos' soldiers, who were still fighting, looked up at him from the ground; they recognized it as the Sikka Brakos had taken, as it had his markings on it that you could see from below. As they watched, Jebel unceremoniously tossed the brightly robed and bloodied body of Brakos and then his two crew members out of the Sikka like worthless debris.

The soldiers stared blankly for several moments, then dejectedly threw their weapons down and held their hands up in surrender, staring in shock at the place where their leader's lifeless body lay in a heap, watching the Sikka fly away with its new pilot. It had been so sudden they could hardly believe it, but it was true. Brakos was gone, and those who followed him would pay the price for having been so foolish. They had betrayed their people by following the wrong person, by seeking personal gain above honor, and all who made that decision would deeply regret it.

Once the news reached the troops, they lost their passion and laid down their arms. The remaining stolen Sikka Manu had surrendered quickly to the superior Ryzen flyers. The fleet of 400 Theralonain ships was now a fleet of about 120, the ones that had turned away and headed home. Within a few hours, the fires were out, although it would take many months to repair all the damage. The war was over.

Chapter 14

"The leader who brings out greatness in the soldiers gains importance. In no other way is a leader measured."

From the Tome of the Ryzen

Heedless of the noise around them, Lupo and Maz stumbled their way from the landing pad to the healers' hall. Although it was only a matter of minutes, by the time they reached the doors Maz was nearly unconscious. Healers in the traditional light yellow robes ran out of the doors and carried Maz into the building, laying him on a raised, wheeled bed. They shoved Lupo aside as they worked, busy with the task of saving his life.

From their talk, Lupo realized the cut was very near to an important blood carrier in the thigh. The healers called it the "heart of the leg", which meant nothing to Lupo but it sounded serious. Had he done the right thing tying off the leg with his belt? As if they could hear his thoughts, or perhaps he had spoken aloud in his distress, a junior healer turned to him and said, "You probably saved his life with that belt. Now go rest. We've got this." Relieved, Lupo backed away and leaned against the nearest wall out of the healers' way.

A young woman burst through the doors. "I saw a Sikka land. Was a Ryzen hurt? Is it my brother?"

The healer who had spoken to Lupo stopped her.

"If you're talking about the young man on the bed, you'll have to get out of the way so we can help him. Go stand over here with this other Ryzen. He brought him in. You can keep each other company."

The woman turned to look at Lupo. He had seen her before; it was Tahari, Maz's sister. When he brought news of Draq's death she had been silent and withdrawn, almost stunned; now, she was weeping, her vest showing signs of burns and blood on the surface. He introduced himself again, and she nodded as if she remembered, which was probably courtesy rather than recollection; she was nearly frantic.

"So it was Maz; you brought him in? You were with him? What happened?"

Lupo told her as much as he knew. He described the fight to her, including Maz's last words to Brakos. She smiled through her tears.

"I'm glad he said that to him," she said. "I'll be sure to tell my parents. Once we know that he'll be alright I'll go and tell them. They don't know anything. I heard people saying Brakos was dead and that Maz killed him, and then someone said Maz was hurt or dead. I had to come and find out."

"I understand," said Lupo. "He's your brother."

"Baby brother," she said, her eyes filling with tears again. "He's two hands of years younger than I am. I can't get used to thinking of him as grown up. I helped my mother take care of him when he was little. He was such a cute baby! So chubby …"

"I'm sure he was. He's not a baby now, Tahari. He fought well, like a Ryzen. He helped end the war and save thousands from slaughter. You can be very proud of him."

"I am. I just want to be able to tell him that myself."

"I believe you will. The healers are very good. They know what they're doing."

As they waited for word Tahari told Lupo stories of Maz as a child, and of her own growing-up years, why she decided to become a teacher, what her changing hopes were for the future. He, in turn, told her a little of his life and dreams, about his path in the Ryzen, everything he could think of, until he began to lose track of the time.

After a while, Jebel came walking down the hall towards them. "Is Maz going to be all right?" he asked.

"We are waiting for word." Lupo and Tahari simultaneously responded in unison, and turned to look at each other. In any other situation they probably would have shared a laugh too but not now.

"Well good, but we need to get back, chief; the fighting is going well, but the fleet is still out there," Jebel replied.

"You're right, Jeb," Lupo responded.

He turned to Tahari, taking her hand and speaking softly. "We must get back to our Sikka; I will be back as soon as I can."

Just then, a grey-haired man in healer robes came out to talk with them.

"Well, he'll recover," the healer said. "He's resting now. We gave him something to make him sleep. You can see him, but don't wake him. He's patched up, but he lost a lot of blood. That's something we can't quickly replace. We have medicines to make blood faster, but he has to drink a lot of water and rest more than usual because it's a drain on his energy. That's going to take time. Let him sleep now. When he wakes we'll give him food and water. You can wait if you like, or you can go tell his parents or any other family he has. It sounds like the fighting has stopped. We don't hear everything in here. Someone said the enemy leader was killed. Is that true?"

"Yes," said Lupo. "You just patched up the Ryzen who killed him. Good work."

The healer was amazed, and said he would tell everyone who they had in their hall. He would make sure Maz would get extra special attention. Lupo and Tahari thanked him and told him they would return soon, after bringing the news to Maz's parents. Lupo and Jebel headed to the waiting sikka on the landing pad and departed.

Tahari went to her mother to tell her what had happened. Tamu was waiting outside the trauma ward where Bahi was treating injured citizens. Tahari ran and hugged her father, "Maz was stabbed but he is going to be fine." She began to recount the tale that Lupo had told her about the battle with Brakos and about how brave her little brother had been. They agreed they would wait briefly there for Bahi to finish her duties before they gave her the news.

When Bahi was finished, she came out to her waiting family and they told her all about Maz. She was astonished to hear what had happened in the battle, and was thankful for the information the Ryzen healers had given to Tahari, especially the assurance that he would be fine when he woke up. As a healer herself, she understood the situation, but as a mother she still shed a tear.

"Well, I must go see my boy. I don't care if he is sleeping."

They all headed off to the healer hall to see Maz. Bahi stayed at his side and held his hand for the next few hours. Lupo arrived back to check on Maz and introduced himself to Tamu and Bahi. They happily greeted him and thanked him for helping save their son's life.

A few minutes later, War Chief Cree entered the room to check on his Ryzen and the warrior who defeated Brakos--the hero who also happened to be his nephew. Maz was still sleeping and wouldn't wake for several hours, according to the healers, so he talked with his brother and sister briefly to tell them how proud he was of his nephew and how he had proven himself to be a true Ryzen.

Cree turned to Lupo.

"Squadron Chief, I am pleased with your performance, especially your leadership and actions in battle and for the excellent job he did training the new Ryzen, Maz.

Lupo was surprised and honored. "War Chief, thank you for your kind words. I did my job, sir."

"Well,that's what we expect of a Ryzen. Now, since the battle only just ended, there is still much work for the War Chief of the nine tribes to do. I must get to work."

He bid his family goodbye and ordered the Ryzen healers to continue to look after Maz and to let him know of his nephew's progress.

"After I leave here, I have a meeting with the Sages. We have many decisions to make. How will we prevent a surprise attack in the future? Will we be less trusting of our allies in the future? Will we be more mindful of the risk of wild ranting by loudmouths? Plans must be made. We must consult the Grandmothers, as well. They will see what we might miss. A Ryzen team will be sent to offer surrender terms; when they return successfully, we will construct peace terms that will hopefully last longer. I'll be back after I attend to these matters."

After Cree had left, Tamu realized they needed to go check on their residence to see if it was still livable and not burned. Maz wqould be sleeping for some time so they invited Lupo to join them for something to eat, and he politely accepted.

They walked in companionable silence, taking in all the damage and carnage that the attacks of the day had left on their citadel and giving thanks to the Creator that it hadn't been worse. Once back at Tamu and Bahi's quarters, they noticed there was some fire damage to the outside areas, but their quarters were on the inside of a cluster of round stone dome-shaped rooms called aiglus that made up the alayas, or residences. They had five domes surrounding a central area called a lana. A passageway led from the exterior walkways into the lana, and each dome opened on to the lana, closed off with close-fitting doors that prevented the fires from entering the domes themselves. There were scorch marks on the stone floor of the lana, but it appeared the fire had been smothered successfully. Bahi was upset that her lovely gardens were all gone, but the rest was fine. More important to Tamu, all his research was unscathed.

They were thankful. The war was over, Maz was the hero of the day, and he would be able to return home soon to rest and recover. Lupo and Tahari sat down to eat with Tamu and Bahi, who sensed a growing relationship between their daughter and the Ryzen and were pleased. Once again, Lupo heard stories about Maz as a child, about the funny things he said and the tricks he played on others, and laughed. This was a good family, a solid family, and their relief and joy that Maz would be all right was wonderful to see. He heard stories about Maz and Tahari's brother, Draq, and comforted the parents with the news that Maz had brought an end to Draq's killer with Draq's own knife. It would never completely ease the pain of loss, but it was at least a small comfort.

After the meal, they went in a group back to see their young hero. They found him awake but very tired. He was sipping broth through a slim tube, pausing only to take a breath. A healer fed him a type of porridge with a spoon in between sips. His task for the next day was resting and producing more blood. He would not be allowed to go home for two days, if then. Maz was glad to hear the war was over, and was eager to hear about what his uncle Cree had said to them. He listened intently to all the news and even discussed Theralonian politics. Maz was feeling much better after his long sleep and whatever the healers had given him.

"I wish I could force the Theralonians to change a few things," said Tahari as she looked at her brother's tired face. "Did you know there are no women in their fighting forces? No women in their Assembly? Almost no women business owners? It's absurd. The men couldn't possibly think they're capable of running a country on their own! Most men can't even find their … um, their dinner without help!"

"I resent that," said Lupo, laughing. "I can find my dinner easily. I just go to a cook shop or dinner house, and there it is!"

"You know what I meant," Tahari said.

"Yes, I do. Dinner wasn't the word you had in mind, was it?"

"No, it wasn't, but I couldn't say what I really meant in front of my baby brother."

"Your baby brother is a national hero. I'd think there's not much you could say that would shock him."

"You may be right," Tahari said. "I guess my brother has grown up, after all."

Maz shook his head as they both laughed. That admission from his sister was almost worth all the pain to Maz. She thought he had grown up? It was about time! If only it hadn't taken a war to bring that about!

Matay fought well in the battle, and his companions with him. The morning after the battle, they had gone on a diplomatic mission. They were said to be preparing to return with two other Sikka Manu to reopen the embassy, negotiate terms with the Assembly of Delegates, and try to put the war behind them. It would not be easy; the Delegates had certainly been duped by Brakos, but it was hard to overlook the consequences of their foolishness. While it was better to attribute the errors of Nesos to stupidity rather than malice, it was undeniable that some of the Delegates were in agreement with Brakos or simply wanted to get in on the profits he had assured them were to be gained through a war. His crew didn't envy Matay the job of walking that narrow path. Still, if anyone could do it, the Ryzen was the one who could make it happen. His years in the service of his homeland as ambassador to foreign countries had taught him much about understanding other cultures and working with their differences. If he could gently steer them in a better direction, he would do so, but the policy of the Grandmothers was always in the direction of suggestion and guidance rather than force.

Nesos City, Theralona, the next day.

The sun reflected off the ocean's surface, shimmering in the morning light. Matay, Sidu and Dalini were flying over the ocean again; this time they flew eastward, along with the two Sikka Manu, Flying Serpent and Stalking Lion, for added security returning to Nesos from Tambak Citadel. It felt like just hours after the battle at the gates of the Citadel, and they barely were given time to change into clean clothes before the Grandmothers ordered them to fly back and "tell these fools what their folly will cost them". Their mission was to convince the Assembly of the truth of what they had learned about the real motivation for the war, in the hope that the war would indeed be over and not continue beyond the tragedy that had already happened.

They brought a witness to help with persuasion. The prisoner of war, Miros, had been an accomplice of Brakos until he found out what Brakos was really doing. It was one thing to call for political equality, and another to seize political power for personal gain. The attack on coastal villages completely turned Miros away from supporting the insurgents, and Matay was certain he was completely turned away from his former support of the late Brakos' violent movement. The moment Brakos died Miros dropped on one knee and swore loyalty to Matay, who found it extremely embarrassing. Of course, he made use of it anyway, and Miros was along for the ride, mostly to testify about what Brakos had been up to.

Matay relaxed into the flight. No one to challenge them in the air; the three stolen Sikka Manu were recaptured. He could simply fly, enjoying the journey back to the city he left so hurriedly a hand of days earlier, and in such turmoil. Their reception was likely to be unfriendly, but he was determined to remain calm and flow like the waters of the ocean, even with the need for haste. The day would unfold as it would, and each moment brought its own challenges.

Right now, his most critical challenge was staying awake to fly the Sikka. He hadn't slept much. There were only three seats in a Sikka, so Miros sat on the floor between Sidu and Dalini. Matay had been tense since Brakos first began his campaign, when he was stirring people to hatred and anger. Now that he was gone, the Ryzen and Timor Laut were hopeful Nesos would return to normal and his work as Ambassador would go smoothly once again.

The coast of Theralona came in sight, its white-columned buildings gleaming. As they approached the city, however, they saw a different picture. The streets of Nesos were filled with rioters, mobs screaming, brandishing sticks and throwing rocks. The Sikka's sensors made their shouts perfectly clear. It was apparently not enough for every adult male to have the vote; now they demanded a stipend paid to every voter from the city's treasury. The rioters weren't subtle or quiet about their demands. Of course, they wanted the wealthy taxed heavily to support the stipend. They demanded a share of the loot they supposed they would get from the war on Timur Laut; it was evident the news of the defeat of the Theralonian army and the death of Brakos hadn't reached them yet. Matay flew silently, high above the mob, trying not to swear on hearing what they said through the sensitive sound receptors built into the Sikka and transmitted to him through the Ichak. How could anyone reach these fools? Timur Laut had won a battle, but these unruly crowds were likely to demand a continuation of the war, wanting the riches Brakos had promised.

Matay enhanced the sound transmission so that it could be heard by the others in the Sikka. Miros was astonished to hear the voices from so far below, and then he realized what they were saying as they shouted in the local language.

"Fools!" he said. "They probably won't even listen to us! They'll keep rioting in the streets, wanting riches that don't exist. Will the Delegates be able to talk sense into them? Will we be able to reach them?"

"Probably not," Matay agreed. "But we'll do our best. It's not our fault if they destroy themselves. We can mourn, but it's as the book of the Wisdom of the Grandmothers says. 'Against stupidity, even the Eternal struggles in vain.'"

He landed on the roof of the Assembly Hall, which was high enough that the Sikka could not be seen from the street. He locked it down securely, and limited access to himself and his crew. No other Ichak could be used to activate the vehicle, no matter how high-ranking the wielder. If the three of them were killed, their Sikka was a lump of metal that would explode if there was an attempt to break into it. The three Ryzen brought their Ichaki and, with Miros following, descended a little-known stairway from the roof directly down to the servants' passageway behind the kitchen.

No one was doing any cooking at the moment. The kitchen staff were elsewhere, possibly hiding in the basement. Matay had regularly paid lower level employees for information about the day to day workings of the building. One never knew when that kind of knowledge would prove to be useful. Following the drawings he had made and memorized years ago, and updated regularly, Matay led his group through the service hallways to the side entrance of the large meeting hall.

As he had expected, most of the Delegates were there, and had apparently brought their families for safety, since there were women and children in the room huddled against the walls. It was strange to see a society where women were excluded from government; perhaps that was why their society was so much behind Timur Laut. Women looked to the future, which is why grandmothers made the major decisions in Timur Laut. They bore the children, helped raise the grandchildren and great-grandchildren, and because they knew the past and cared about the future they were the best guardians of the people's well-being. Men were action oriented, as his mother had often told him, and sometimes would do something wrong just to be doing something. Timur Laut's political system, in which men generally dealt with immediate issues and women had the long view, made sense to him. He had served as ambassador in Theralona, and before that in Tenifra, Borea, and a brief assignment in Songha. He preferred his own land's system to any other. Now, it was his job to keep his land safe from idiots who thought only of looting and free meals.

He stepped into the room, with his companions behind him. Pitching his voice so it would carry, he shouted in the kana dialect, "Men of Nesos! The war is over!" He repeated it until the room was silent and people were staring at him. With the chatter stilled, he continued.

"You know me. I am Matay, Ambassador to your fair land from Timur Laut. Your army attacked our capital city and was defeated yesterday. Brakos, who fomented this war, is dead. I bring peace terms. Hear me and do well. Refuse to listen and live in hunger and pain. Your decision."

"Impossible!" shouted a tall, thin man Matay recognized as Improbus, a troublemaking Delegate from the inland mountains. "No one could sail a ship from Timur Laut in only one day! He lies!"

"Well, of course I didn't come in a ship!" Matay's exasperation was obvious. "I flew." And so they would take notice, he used the repeller action in his Ichak to lift him up about three cubits into the air. High enough for everyone to see, but not so high as to make himself an easy target for an ambitious archer. He heard their gasps, and lowered himself back to the ground.

"What I can do in this room, my flyer can do in the sky and over the sea. Some of you know this. Some of you saw me leave last week in my flyer! Have you forgotten already?"

The room was silent. Obviously, they remembered.

Matay went on. "I heard the citizens out in the street. I see you have wisely brought your families here for safety. Your enemy of the moment is not my nation, not my people. It's your own people, who want to be given what they did not earn and take what they do not deserve. You must decide if you want us as an ally or as a conqueror. I am willing to go either way. Hear me and follow my suggestions, and you might get your country back. Ignore me, and perish. Unlike you, I have studied the history of many nations, and I assure you these mobs will not simply go home."

Another man raised his voice. "Why are you willing to be an ally? We attacked your country!"

"Yes, Agricolos, some of your people did. We are officially considering them a rogue group in rebellion against your government. Your legitimate government is not responsible for their actions. Your senator Brakos is dead. Many of his cohort are also dead. I have here one Miros, who is one of you and will tell you more about what Brakos has been doing. Then I will present my people's offer to you, and you may decide what path you will take."

Miros stepped forward and spoke to the Delegates and their families, explaining the extent of Brakos' plotting. He told them how Brakos attacked the coast of Timur Laut, pretending it was by orders of the Assembly; he told them of Brakos' men dressing up like the Timur, with brown stain and wigs, to make the people of Guayota Cor and the rest of Tenifra think that Timur laut had attacked them. He explained how Brakos had already become rich through shrewd manipulation of Nesos trade markets, and planned to become still richer by deceiving people into supporting a war that would put endless sums into his own pockets. By the time he was finished, the delegates were wishing Brakos was still alive so they could kill him themselves.

The delegate called Improbus stepped up to Miros. "Lies! Brakos was from my own district. He was a fine man, an honest man. He would never do those things! Your report is false!" He attempted to grab Miros by the shoulders.

Dalini was instantly at his side, touching his Ichak against Delegate Improbus' ankle. The man fell to the ground, unable to pick himself up. The harder he tried, the more he was pulled to the ground, until he was lying flat on the floor groaning.

"I guess Heavyweight works on politicians," said Dalini softly in his own language. To the group he said loudly in kana, "The weight of his foolishness will hold him for a while. Now let the wiser ones talk."

The delegates discussed, argued, shouted, and eventually voted. They voted to accept Timur Laut's generous offer of cease-fire while they discussed the terms of an alliance, and also voted to overturn the illegal vote to extend the vote to every man in the city. They voted, instead, for heads of households with two or more children to have the right to vote provided they had completed the basic level of education and paid their taxes. It was a compromise they had previously rejected, and Matay thought it showed they had learned something in the last week. Perhaps they would let the women vote next.

Chapter 15

"It is impossible for the fools to tread the path of learned ones."

~ prophecy of the nine Grandmothers

Twelve Days Later, Nesos City

After a quick journey home to report to the Grandmothers, the ambassadorial team returned to the Assembly Hall. The return to Nesos was much easier this time than the previous trip. Instead of sneaking into the Assembly Hall, Matay and his team proceeded through the streets openly, the entire diplomatic mission was made up of Ryzen. The war was over, but it was too soon to consider this a safe post. There were people who still thought Timur Laut had attacked Theralona, even though all the evidence was to the contrary. Evidence didn't matter to some people if it contradicted the story they had made up. For many of the "Equality Party", their story of oppressive Timur Laut ruthlessly invading innocent Theralona to steal its gold was just too appealing, and the fact that it was completely false was irrelevant.

The nine Ryzen walked steadily up the marble stairway to the entrance doors of the Hall. The people in the portico moved aside, and they entered the main receiving area, then continued to the Delegates' auditorium. When they walked into the auditorium, there was a hush; Matay continued on to stand in front of the Presiding Delegate's podium, while the rest lined up behind him.

"Ambassador Matay," the Presiding Delegate said. "You honor us with your presence."

"Yes, I do," Matay said, addressing them in return in the kana language. "I'm happy to be here in such different circumstances from our last meeting."

Since the last meeting was in the middle of the war and had not been exactly friendly, there was an awkward moment until Matay spoke again.

"I bring good news, however. I have the terms of alliance given by the Nine Grandmothers. I think you will find them extremely merciful."

He looked around the room. "In case any of you have forgotten, a fleet of your boats filled with fighters, as well as three flyers stolen from us, attacked our capital city last week and dropped fire on our residential areas, where there are children. Perhaps you don't value children; we do. Your people had previously attacked villages, killing innocent people. There was also an attack on Tenifra by people disguised as people of Timur Laut, with brown stain on their skin and dark wigs on their heads. We know that wasn't just a fashion choice, delegates; it was an attempt to deceive the people of Tenifra, so they would think Timur Laut was behind the attack. To summarize, you have killed our people, destroyed a significant portion of our capital city, and slandered us with a false story and an attack on another nation. What do you think our leaders will do to you? Presiding Delegate, what would you do if someone did these things to you? What requirements would you make before making a treaty of friendship?" Matay's voice was firm, but not strident; he seemed to have no emotion at all, not anger or grief.

The Presiding Delegate hesitated before speaking.

"I would need assurances that it would not happen again. Perhaps we would maintain an army in the land of a people who did that. We would almost certainly execute their leaders, and take all the gold in their treasury."

"And is that what you think we should do to you?"

"Well … it would be your right."

"Then it's a good thing for you we aren't incredibly foolish, isn't it?"

There was a gasp in the auditorium, from many throats; had the Ambassador really called them foolish?

Apparently he had. "Do you think we don't know this was the work of a rogue who was running the operation for his own profit? Some of you in this room went along with it, for reasons known only to you. I can ask what you were thinking, but I really don't care. That is the difference between us, delegates. I care about actions and facts, not emotion and innuendo. What actually happened is that you had an out-of-control criminal running your war policy, you believed everything he said without verification, and you got caught up in the emotional furor of the fantasy he sold you. Free food. Free money. Riches from looting. Yes, I think that was incredibly foolish, even dangerously so, and that's all the explanation I need.

"It was all the Grandmothers needed, too. Hear this: the Nine Grandmothers rule with wisdom and foresight. They do not rule in order to fill their pockets with trash. They rule to create better lives for their people. Here is their demand.

"You caused damage to our capital city. The damage must be paid for. You will agree to pay the bill for damages within three dozen days of receiving it. That's one month and six days by your customary calendar. The bill will be the actual cost of the materials to rebuild, plus the cost of labor for any skilled workers hired to do the rebuilding. No one will profit from this, other than the fair profit from honest trade made by the suppliers of material. If we find that your people have played false with the calculations and made personal profit, even if it is cheating your own people, we will levy a penalty of three times the cost of materials, to be paid from the pockets of Delegates in equal shares.

"As to the unskilled labor, you will provide that also. All the prisoners we have taken will do the work of rebuilding our city, since they caused the damage. This will help them understand the consequences of their actions. We hope it will teach them a simple lesson that we teach to our children: don't break other people's things. It's not nice. The ones who caused the damage will do the work of fixing what they have broken. So say the Grandmothers.

"Furthermore, after the repairs to the city are done, the prisoners will make right the other kinds of damage they have done. Many families lost a parent in the battle. When a parent is gone, in addition to grieving, the families struggle with keeping up the home as well as earning the money needed for expenses. Sometimes both parents earned income, and that needs to be replaced. Therefore, the prisoners will either work as servants in these households until all the children are grown, to make up for the damage they have done, or if they have skills they will work for an employer in the city and give half their pay to the families of the deceased. If they act with bad faith in any way, they will spend the rest of their lives in holding cells under the Hall of the Grandmothers.

"Furthermore, any of you here in this city, or even in this hall, who have profited from your involvement in this war, will also go to Timur Laut and work to rebuild the city, make right the damage, and labor to help the families you have harmed. We have your names. You may not appeal, unless you have absolute proof that you were not involved in profiteering. In that case, the ones who accused you falsely will pay the price.

"Do you have any questions?"

No one spoke at first. Then Delegate Agricolos from the farming region stepped forward.

"Why are you not requiring our lives, or the lives of our families?" he asked. "It is what we would have done in your place."

"I already told you," Matay said. "We're not foolish. What value do we gain from your deaths? Here we gain recompense and labor. We are made whole again. What more do we need? What is the value of a death? We value life. We seek just consequences, not excessive punishment. The Grandmothers believe this lesson will be more effective than frightening you with a host of bodies displayed on the city walls, which is more your way of intimidating your enemies. We seek to teach, not to merely frighten."

The discussions continued, with matters such as delivery of the bills, transporting the ones in Nesos who would go to Tambak City to work, and other details being resolved. Every delegate eventually had something to say, and Matay's companions were assigned to help with the work, take notes, write orders, and all the mundane duties that governments require. It was late when they finally were settled in the embassy tower, able to have food and rest. The morning would come soon enough.

As they left the embassy common room for their sleeping chambers, Dalini commented to Sidu, "That was a bit of a disappointment."

"In what way?" asked Sidu. "I thought it went well. The ambassador is skilled with words, and he got their signatures on the contracts without any great difficulty. What did you find disappointing?"

"It went too well," Dalini said. "I didn't get to use Heavyweight even once today."

Sidu laughed. "You're always unexpected, Dalini. I can count on you to have a different view of everything. At least you're never boring."

Coming up behind them, Matay laughed. "I realize using force against these idiots would have been satisfying, boys. Unfortunately, we're diplomats. We have to use words. Weapons are a last resort. Now, go to your chambers and get some rest. The sunrise will come at the usual time. I don't want to see half-asleep scribes when we get started copying all those agreements in the morning!"

His companions groaned and shuffled off to their sleeping chambers, dreading the long hours of copying ahead of them.

A Month Later

Tambak City

The days and weeks went by in Tambak City. A coalition of Ryzen, University associates, and Guildhall members supervised the cleanup and rebuilding of the firebombed areas. People began healing, from physical wounds as well as those of mind or spirit. Once released by the healers, Maz trained daily, determined to gain back any edge he might have lost in the weeks he was lying in bed with his leg elevated. Cree worked with him whenever possible, but Lupo was responsible for training him, so he did most of the hard work.

At one training session, Maz had some questions for Lupo. He had come to admire the older Ryzen a great deal, especially after seeing him in battle. Lupo's interest in Tahari had brought him to the Kau family home on many occasions, so that he was beginning to seem like one of them. It seemed natural to share his thoughts with him.

"Ryzen," he said, following the common form of speaking to a fellow Ryzen, "I've been wondering about something." He paused in his workout to do some stretches while talking.

"What's that?"

"I've been looking at things differently since... well, you know."

"Since the battle?"

Maz nodded. "It seems like everything looks different to me. Like, for example, this award we're getting. The gold feather. It just seems... well, not quite wrong, but just... not right."

"I understand, and I agree. I don't feel I deserve an award for just doing my job. That would be like giving a clerk an award for adding up numbers correctly!"

"That's it exactly. I've been seeing how every bit of my training led me to that battle. It's why we train physically, not just mentally. Mental and spiritual training would enable us to work with wailu kile, to use our Ichak, everything. We train physically so we can win a physical challenge, like a hand to hand fight in battle. Every drill is about battle. Our sparring and grappling matches are about battle. That's what I prepared for, for months. I trained hard, and it worked. I was ready when I needed to be. Why does that deserve an award? The training deserves the award, not me!"

"You're right. But the only way to reward the training, to tell the people that our Way is effective, is to reward us. The feathers are really for the ones who came before us. They're for all our trainers and the ones who trained them, to thank them for teaching us the physical aspects of the Way. Wearing those feathers is part of the job. When you walk down the street with the feathers on your capaicha, you're saying, "I've got this. I'm here and I'm ready." It's evidence of one thing; you upheld the legacy."

"Good, I guess that makes sense. Three months ago I would have been so proud to be honored; now, it's different. I was kind of uncomfortable. This helps. Thanks."

Done with his cool down stretches, Maz started trotting back to the training hall to wash and change back into his uniform from the gray loincloth he wore for exercise. Lupo trotted beside him.

"Do you feel uncomfortable about Brakos?"

"No. That was for Draq. It was justice. It was my job, too. It was part of taking care of my family."

"Good. It's not a light thing, ending a life."

"No, it's not. I think it was necessary, not just for vengeance; he was like a rabid dire wolf that needed to be stopped. All the things we learned in the briefings, the things he was doing! It's like killing a poisonous reptile. Necessary. I have no doubt about that."

"I'm glad. If you ever find yourself troubled, you can talk to me."

"I know."

"Now let's get cleaned up. Remember, you're joining us for dinner tonight! And aren't you meeting with Tahari for tea this afternoon?"

"I am. Why?"

"Just making sure your plans haven't changed... brother."

"Never, little brother! I'll race you back to the changing room!"

#   #   #   #   #

Lupo arrived at the tea shop a hand of minutes before the appointed time. He selected a table outside, secluded enough for their conversation to remain private but with a good view of the people passing by. He had noticed Tahari enjoyed watching the crowds, and he wanted her to have everything she wanted today.

She arrived right on time, as he hoped she would. It was a good sign, as she was usually a little bit late. The server came to take their order as soon as Tahari sat down, and they ordered hot tea and a plate of nuts and dried fruits with flat cakes dipped in honey.

After some conversation about the fine weather, Tahari brought up a topic she said had been bothering her.

"I'm concerned about my little brother," she told him. "If he doesn't talk about his troubles, he holds them in his heart until it burns him, like the fire in the heart of a volcano. Can you talk to him about the battle? He killed a man, Lupo. People see a hero, but I see the little baby whose bottom cloths I changed."

"Already done. I talked to him this morning. He was able to talk about his concerns and resolve them. No need to change his bottom cloths, my flower. I have done it for you."

"You are a very competent man," she said.

"Just doing my job, taking care of junior Ryzen. But it's not all to my credit. He already knew he had done right."

"How can you be certain?"

"He and I were both in a Ryzen briefing about the extent of Brakos' evil deeds. He knew what kind of man it was who killed his brother and tried to kill him too."

"Was there more, besides bringing the battle to our shores?"

"Yes, there was. He belonged to the followers of a deranged group, who sacrifice children on a burning altar. He wanted to require all of Theralonia to worship him and his group. Every family would have to sacrifice their firstborn child. No exceptions.

"He became rich from the buying and selling of slaves. He sold people as if they were livestock, like selling a pig or a chicken. Young girls were sold to be used as playthings. It's bad enough that women in Theralona have no voice in society; he denied them control of their own lives.

"Everyone knows he was profiteering, making money from the war, encouraging his soldiers to loot the places they would capture. Now we know more of his evil deeds, and the names of the people who ran these atrocities with him. Maz knows he executed a vile, disgusting criminal for the sake of protecting our people. He has no guilt; it was like killing a deadly reptile, nothing more."

She smiled. "I'm glad. I thank you for helping my little brother. How can I help you in return?"

Her smile was all the thanks Lupo needed. Encouraged, he went on.

"I have a concern deep in my heart as well, you know. Shall I share it?" Tahari smiled and nodded.

"I am alone. My parents have gone on the sky journey, and until I set sail myself I will not see them anymore. I have no brothers. I will have lived three dozen years next summer. I have no wife, because I have never found a woman who asked me. I have a small house near the Hall of the Ryzen, which I let out for a good rental fee. I have a deposit with the goldsmith. I own a small coconut grove that brings a nice income each year. How can I enjoy this if I have no one to share it with me? I am puzzled, my flower. What can be the solution to my problem?"

He watched her carefully. Had he been too bold? It was inappropriate for a man to suggest marriage to a woman; that was for the woman to do, as the future mother and grandmother of his household. Would she feel insulted?

She smiled and shook her head.

"That is a serious problem, my dear friend. I am not certain what to suggest. The young girls whose mothers and grandmothers are arranging marriages for them are too young and timid. They will be afraid of a seasoned Ryzen warrior like you! And the older widows will want young men with pink cheeks who will flatter them and pick fruit for them. They want to be pampered, and they want a man's attention. The Ryzen Way must always be first for you.

"It's a problem, my friend. I only see one solution. You must find a woman with a few years in a profession or trade, who has lived... oh... perhaps two dozen and four years under the sun. She should have parents, and perhaps a brother, so that you would immediately have a family.

"Where will you find such a woman?" Her eyes shone as she looked deep into his soul. Her voice deepened with emotion.

"I don't know," he said, "but I know the saying; the Way is strong and has no hindrance. If my way leads to such a wonderful woman as you describe, it will happen. She will speak to me."

"I am speaking to you, Lupo. I see you. I have a house also, near my parents. It has only three aiglus around the lana, but there is room for more. Maz and I have lost a brother. My parents have lost a son. Will you be a husband to me, a brother to Maz, and a son to my parents?"

His voice shaking, he said softly, "I will."

"Then come to my parents and I will ask my mother to add you to our family."

They gazed into each other's eyes—the only intimacy permitted in public. Lupo placed a woven strip on the table, to pay for the tea and food, and they walked out of the tea house together into a new life.

Twelve Days Later

The trio of musicians stood in an alcove off the central atrium. Soft drums, flute, and gourd blended skillfully together, creating a festive mood all around Maz's family dwelling. Tables with refreshments occupied the walls, and guests in their best attire mingled, are, drank, and talked. The Kau family were celebrating the return to normal life.

Tamu and Cree were discussing their respective jobs. Cree now held the title of Defense Chief, reporting directly to the Grandmothers. Tamu, of course, still remained at the University in the department of Star Studies. He was speaking eloquently about his latest discovery.

"I tell you, brother, this thing is coming closer and closer! I don't know what it is or how close it's going to pass to our earth, but it's moving incredibly fast. I've consulted with sea navigators, and they say they can see it with their farseeing glasses. Ours is much more powerful, but isn't it amazing that it can be seen with the hand held models out on the sea?"

"Certainly, Tamu. That's amazing. An object of some kind moving across the sky? And you think it will get closer?"

"Yes, I do. Maybe we'll be able to see it without a glass!"

"Do you think it might come close enough to us to cause trouble?"

"Oh, it's possible, it's happened before, though not for countless generations, so I won't worry about it."

"No, that's my job. Tamu, the moment you think it's going to get too close, you let me know. Promise,"

"Certainly, Cree! I'll tell you the moment it looks like it's headed for us. But what could you do?"

"Consult the Ryzen sages, prepare, inform the Grandmothers, probably. Speaking of which, I have a meeting tomorrow with the Sages and the Grandmothers. It sounds important."

"Your work is so interesting, brother!"

"You look at the stars, and you think my work is interesting?"

"Certainly! You're a hero! You and my son, both. You taught him well, and I'm grateful. By the way, are your wife and daughters here? I'd like to thank them, too."

"They went off with Bahi. Some secret woman thing." Cree looked around the room.

The guests were all dressed in their best, like Tamu and Cree, who wore short, hip length sleeveless tunics, embroidered all over the front. Below the tunic they wore knee length kilts of coconut leaf fiber, interwoven with beads. They both wore shell necklaces and feathered headdresses; each feather represented an honor earned in their profession. Most of the men wore similar headdresses and clothing; the younger men, like Maz and Lupo, wore sleeveless embroidered vests over a bare chest. The women wore close-fitting bodices with sheer, bell-shaped, flattened elbow length sleeves made of plant fibers, worn over slim skirts with fringed hems down to the ankle. They wore elaborate bead and shell necklaces, and their headdresses floated behind them, with feathers mixed with dried flowers.

Most of the women had stepped away from the gathering; now they returned, in a group, their movements like a dance. The crowd applauded; it was traditional to surprise guests with a ceremony, usually a wedding.

Bahi sang out loudly; everyone recognized the melody, and all the women joined in. The words were simple. "We claim a man for our sister."

Cree laughed. "That's what they're up to! Who is it? One of mine?"

"I don't think so, Cree. Look over there."

Cree looked, and Tahari danced slowly into the room. Her dress was vivid red, a color reserved for brides and special occasions. Her hair was a spray of wild dark curls, the feathered headdress balanced on top. Her feet were bare. She danced over to Lupo, who stood, stunned, as if he had never seen her before. In her hands she had a chest plate worked out of bamboo fibers, the traditional representation of a house. She lifted it up; he had to stoop to get underneath, and she fastened it over his shoulders, signifying his willingness to live in her house, under her roof.

She sang: "Beneath my roof may you find peace, and shelter from the storm."

Then he took snow-white shells, the kind used for trade along the coasts and in the islands. He had a large bag full of them, and he took handfuls and filled her open hands until she couldn't hold any more.

Lupo sang: "I bring you all that you might need to keep you safe and warm."

It was done. The guests burst into a raucous cheer. Tahari put her shells back in the bag, which Lupo handed to Maz. Lupo removed the heavy chest plate, and Cree's daughters took it away. The music changed to a fast dance, traditionally danced by the bride and groom over bamboo poles moving in a complicated pattern. The people wielding the poles were, of course, Ryzen, familiar with all kinds of staffs. The poles clanged together, then both struck the ground, and repeated the pattern. It was a challenge for Lupo and Tahari to dance on the moving poles without injury to their ankles, but they did it, to wild applause.

The guests ate and drank till dawn. No one noticed when Lupo and Tahari left the atrium and walked to Tahari's domes and their first night together.

After the guests had gone home, Tamu and Bahi sat with Maz in the family dining room. This room was the center of home life, with a fireplace in the center and a table dominating one side of the room. The other side had groupings of chairs around low tables, convenient for playing table games with round beads and discs on patterned boards. Tonight they sat around the large table, their feet in the recessed pit under the table, their elbows resting on the tabletop as they sipped tea and ate sweet cakes.

"That was a surprise," said Maz. "It was extremely well done, Mother. I don't think anyone suspected a thing. How did you come up with that dress for Tahari?"

"I've had that dress hidden for years, for just such an opportunity. Every mother of a daughter does so. It's hard to come up with a suitable dress without advance planning. I started working on this wedding when she graduated from the Academy."

"A hand of years ago! I never knew you were so devious."

"Your mother constantly surprises me, son," said Tamu.

"I'm finding out women are pretty surprising, in general," Maz said. "Cree has some interesting challenges, with two daughters. My cousins are extremely devious, I can tell you!"

"Cree has quite a job," said Tamu. "Not just the daughters, but his task of keeping our land safe. It's not just warfare; it's all the other challenges to our safety. Natural disasters like fires and floods, of course; and you know about the wild animal control, don't you?"

Maz nodded. "Yes, we talked about it when I was training with him."

"That's a big responsibility. I wonder what the Grandmothers want to talk to him about. He seemed to think it was a serious matter."

"Pa, it's always a serious matter when the Grandmothers are involved. We think ordinary women are devious? I'm sure the

Grandmothers are even more so. Their ways are unfathomable."

"This is true," said Bahi. "You can't figure us ordinary women out; you certainly can't keep up with the Nine!"

"Nor would I want to. I'm glad they have taken on the burden they have, because I know that no mere man could do it so well." Tamu laughed softly.

"I hope I meet a woman who finds me appealing," said Maz. "I'd like to learn more about women, and the best way to learn is by experience. Isn't that right?"

"Yes, but not too soon," Bahi said. "You're still young, and new to the Ryzen. Get your career under way first. Time enough for women. But, mind you don't take too long! I want to be a grandmother soon!"

"I'm sure Lupo and Tahari will consider your wishes," said Tamu, still laughing.

Chapter 16

"Dream dreams and see visions, but anchor them in ultimate reality."

From the Prophecy of the Nine Grandmothers

Tambak Citadel, Timur Laut

The women quietly filed into the room. They changed into the loose, sleeveless robes set out for them on a table. The room was circular, taking up the entirety of the adobe dome. In the center was a sunken fire pit, already burning. Bowls were placed around the pit. When the women were dressed, they approached the fire pit and sat gracefully on their knees, feet tucked under their hips. The women were not young; most had some silver in their dark hair, and one had hair that had gone entirely silver.

Three more women entered, wearing black sarongs tied over the bust. They were members of the Guardians, an elite group within the Ryzen whose job was to guard and protect. Their particular task was to guard the Nine Grandmothers, the rulers of the continent of Ka-Timur Laut and the Western Islands. They were quiet, discreet, and deadly. Their hair was piled on their heads, secured with silver sticks that were sharpened to a point and could pierce leather. Their arms bore knives in sheaths, and their legs each bore a weapon; a short sword on the right leg, an axe on the left. Their boots held concealed blades. No harm would come to the Grandmothers while the Lady Guardians lived.

Once the Grandmothers were seated, the Guardians brought them each a cup containing a steaming liquid. It was a recipe as old as time itself, and the Grandmothers shared the secret of its making with no one. Then, they sprinkled herbs from the bowls on to the fire, until the smoke was richly scented. Then the Guardians left, on the Grandmothers' instructions, to wait outside the door. It was the autumn equinox, a time for visions, and the Grandmothers sought wisdom at this time each year.

The scented fumes rose from the fire as the grandmothers sipped their beverages. Soon, the visions began. The grandmothers stared around the room, as if seeing something beyond human vision. They began to interact with their visions. Some wept. Some called out. Some wailed and shrieked in anguish. One sang a war song, clapping her hands in rhythm, as if stirring warriors to victory. Many rose up and danced around, undulating as if swept by waves, struggling as if they were drowning.

The visions lasted nearly till dawn. At the end, the grandmothers sank back into their sitting positions, exhausted. The Guardians returned to the room as ordered, helped the Grandmothers to their feet, and escorted them to their sleeping chambers. The night of visions had ended. It was time to talk to the people, to share the visions and the prophecy.

The meeting called by the Nine Grandmothers began at the third hour past sunrise. The Grandmothers took their places in the council chamber, resplendent in their formal red and yellow robes trimmed with red, blue, and brown, their feathered headdresses also reflecting the colors of the Four Elements: Water, Earth, Air and Fire. They came from every region; the western islands, the peaceful coast, the frozen north. They traveled here from the Spine and Highlands, the Bloody Mountains, the hidden central valleys. They wore the faces of the forest dwellers, the eastern fisher folk, and the people of the City. When they were seated in a row at the ceremonial table on which rested the Tome of the Ryzen, a black-clad guard sounded a brass gong. The doors opened to admit the Sages, Ryzen with long red vests over plain black tunics and sarongs, symbolizing at once their rank as Sages, their commitment to the Way of Fire, and their role as guardians of wisdom. They sat opposite the Grandmothers, and then the Senior Brown Vests came and sat at their feet. Most of the Senior Browns wore the tricolor of white tunic, blue sarong, and brown vest, but four wore the brown vest over the black tunic and sarong of a Guardian. The Guardians, a title granted to the elite Ryzen who are masters of combat and warfare who divided amongst them the duty of safeguarding the Ryzen way, stood at the end of the row of Sages. One of these, Defense Chief of the East Cree Kau, was extremely apprehensive about the coming meeting. It was the first meeting called by the Nine since the Council of Peace at the conclusion of the war, and Cree wasn't aware of any threat that required the presence of the Guardians.

The Grandmother who sat in the center, representing the People of the Highlands and the Spine, stood to address the Ryzen. She was tall and straight-backed. Her features were sharp as an eagle's, and her eagle's eyes saw every secret of a man's soul. She wore eagle feathers in her headdress, and on her cheeks were the painted runes of war. Her name was Ouray.

"I have seen a vision in the sky and the mountains and in the fire," she said. "I have seen death and destruction, death by earth and water and wind and fire. The Spine will nurture the people who flee to her for safety, if they are brave and strong of breath." She sat down.

Next, the Grandmother of the Western Isles stood up. She was small and round, with a sweet smile and musical voice. Her hair floated behind her like the waves of the sea at night.

"I have seen a vision in the water," she said. "I saw villages and cities and whole kingdoms drowned. I saw them sink beneath the sea, and I saw the sea cover the earth. But my lands will rise; they will be there when the waters recede. Come to me. I will welcome you." Her name was Ka-Moana.

The Grandmother of the Peaceful Coast stood strong as a tree, her silvery hair moving around her face as if moved by a breeze. Her necklace and headdress had wooden beads, shells, and dried leaves. She was wiry and strong, with a firm jaw.

"I saw a vision in the wind," she said. "The mothers cried because they could not find their children. They called, and they did not answer. The trees fell to the ground, broken, drifting. But some will yet live, and bear leaves and fruit. There will yet be fish. Later, much later, come share our home." Her name was Yakama.

Then a very round woman with fur trim on her headdress and tunic stood. Her cheeks were round, her eyes bright. She was gentle of speech, and her lap had held many children.

"I have seen a vision in the ice, reflected like the surface of a still lake. I saw my land torn, my children screaming. I weep tears that flood the rifts. My heart grieves, but I see more. I see the wounded lands heal, the snow fall. There will be children again, and seals and fish to feed them. When the land is healed, join us. We are friendly." Her name was Inuit.

Then the grandmother with the eyes of the coyote stood to speak. Her voice was fraught with anger, and her eyes blazed. "I see a vision in fire, in lands torn by lightning and storms, by earthquakes and spinning winds. My lands will suffer. My children will suffer. But we are strong, and we will be there when the travelers come from the east. We will hold you in the bloody arms of the wounded mountains, and we will heal together. I am strong. I will protect." And her name was Anasazi.

A grandmother rose, lifted as on the wind. She was slim and lean, delicate as a flower, strong as an iron spear. Her hair was dark, with silver streaks that framed her face.

"I have seen it in the wind," she said, and her voice was like a song. "I saw water where there had been farmlands, ocean where there was grazing land. I saw ruin and desolation, and water everywhere. But the water diminished, and subsided, and the land was free again, and it bore grain and fruit and fed the animals and the people. I saw this, I saw this," she sang. Her name was Lakota.

A woman stood, tall, with green leaves in her headdress, her skin like the bark of a tree. "I am forest, I am woodlands," she said. "I hear my children weep and mourn. I have seen death and destruction in the earth, in the ground that nourishes but on that day will kill. I have seen death in the water that feeds the trees. But some of the forest will return. Some will be forever beneath the waves, but there will be forest again, and the people will dwell there after the bad times." Her name was Onondaga.

A Grandmother stood, small and lithe and brown, with many feathers and a robe of red and gold. She had dark green leaves mixed with the feathers in her headdress. She climbed and stood on the table, her small feet bare, and she spoke.

"My people will survive in their inland cities, made from good stone. They will know, for I will tell them, and they will leave the coasts and move to the center, and I tell you a mystery; the inland will become coast, and they will learn to fish as well as hunt. None will know their history, because we have our secrets, and though many will be lost under the water, many will live on mountain tops and will build pyramids to remember how they were saved." And her name was Moya.

Last was a Grandmother in the colors of the elements, the colors of the Ryzen. She was straight and tall, but her sadness was deep, and deep was her grief. She wore many knives, sharp and bright, and there was gold in her headdress.

"My city is lost, my people are destroyed. I have seen this in the wind, in the fire, in the earth, in the water. Shaken, burned, drowned, all my precious children! I will not rise again. I will sleep, and sleep again. And my sister across the water, whose people are ignorant and do not listen to her words, she will be gone. I mourn, and I will not be comforted. Indeed, I have seen death in the water, death in the wind, death in the earth. Buried in water we will be." Then she stood taller, growing stronger with each moment, and said, "But even so, I will rise, and when time immeasurable has passed I will welcome my children back, and we will hunt and fish and grow strong."

And her name was Tsalagi.

All was silent. Then Ouray stood up again.

"We have told you our visions. And, Sages and Browns and Guardians, we have a mission for you, the gravest you have known.

Hear this prophecy, which was granted to us by the Creator, the Great Spirit who illuminates the universe, who will someday walk among the people of the earth for a season. This is a true prophecy, which we share with you so that some may live. These things we speak of have happened before and will happen again.

Sages, you will ponder these visions and the prophecy, and seek to understand their meaning. You will determine what must be done to preserve the knowledge our people have gained, and what we inherited from our ancestors before the beginning of this age. It is for you to make a plan so that our culture is not lost. The Ryzen will aid you in this great endeavor. We will tell you more as it is revealed to us, and as you are able to understand.

Now, hear this prophecy. Memorize it. Learn what it means. Tell the people, especially the Ryzen and their families. This is your most important task."

And Ouray recited the prophecy, written in the traditional way used for prophetic utterances since the beginning of their history.

This will come to pass.

Watch for the signs and seasons

Before the chaos.

Evil minded men

Hungry for gold and bloodshed

Will start a false wars.

The Ryzen rise up

Above the burning city

Balance wins the day.

Before the earth-dance

Seven around the bright sun

The end of days comes

The dragon's tail burns

The waters cover the gates

And we are no more.

The high mountain spine

Center of the vast fair land

Go there, Ryzen, fly.

Take women, children

Flee to the center, the heart

And find safety there.

Go westward in boats

Find islands in the sunset

With fruit and fishes

From the spine, go south

Until the seasons go mad

And change their places

The east is not safe.

The plotters of the false war

Have doomed their island.

Waves rule overhead

They flee eastward, middle earth,

An ocean between

Go westward, in dark.

All that walk upon the land

Take boats, and go west.

Save the history.

Save the wisdom of mankind.

Keep it safe from harm.

Chapter 17

"The Cycle of Time continues and returns to its source, where it begins anew."

From the Prophecy of the Nine Grandmothers

Tambak Citadel, Timur Laut

Winter was settling in. Maz was training every day, learning more than he ever expected. As he learned physical techniques, his understanding and wisdom also grew. He learned the history of the Ryzen as well, and was humbled to be part of this brotherhood that existed for so many centuries and was spread over all the regions of the world.

Lupo and Tahari were doing well, continuing in their jobs. Tahari was a skilled teacher of the young, an honored position in Timur Laut; Lupo was a Ryzen, equally honored in his own professional circles, even though not everyone in the community understood what the Ryzen did for them. Still, they had important work, and their shared commitment to their work and to the future of their community made a strong bond between them. Even if Tahari pursued a growing interest in healing, which Maz suspected she would be doing soon, that commitment to the future of their people would always be a bond between them. Maz was happy for them; he hoped someday he could meet a woman who might want him. But where would he find a woman who shared his interests? Warrior-pilots, his assigned specialty, were mostly men. There were a few women, and they were formidable. They were good fighters, good pilots, and generally good at whatever they attempted.

Maz had about another month of pilot training, and then he would be assigned a permanent post. Six more months, and he expected he would have command of his own crew. Ryzen training never stopped; he would be training all his life, striving to better himself. He was running one cold morning just before the winter solstice when he encountered Cree, who was also running on the pathways that circled around at the base of the Mound.

"Uncle!" he said. "Greetings! Will you and your family be joining us for solstice celebrations next week?

Cree slowed a bit until he was running next to Maz.

"I believe so. The women are arranging it. I just go where I'm told."

"They're confusing, aren't they? Women, I mean."

Cree laughed. "You'll get used to them, I promise. They're people, just as we are. You aren't confused by your mother, are you?"

"Constantly, but she's my mother." Cree responded with laughter.

"You always say something unexpected, nephew. What are you doing today?"

"I have my tuition duties. My Ryzen training and the University lectures. I'm cleaning up three streets this evening."

"Good. That's an excellent duty. Builds muscles and character. I used to hate getting assigned to catalogue scrolls. I thought that was the worst, until I had to go find some that had been buried underground, and the cavern collapsed on me. It took a full day to get me out, and I rolled the old scrolls into a breathing tube. I found those scrolls very useful! Many years later, I understood knowledge is never wasted, it just may take time to be useful, as I found out." Cree remembered his student days vividly, and was willing to share those memories freely.

They continued running around the winding path, and when the long circuit was completed they cooled down, stretched, and walked back to the training hall. After a quick wash, Maz went to his duty station, got his supplies, and began cleaning the streets on his designated block. Every student had to pay tuition for education, whether at the University or with the Ryzen, and the tasks to be done to pay tuition were assigned every change of season. Street cleaning was one of the most physically demanding, which Maz enjoyed and even made a game out of it but latrine duty was the thing he truly disliked.

No one had to take that duty more than once a year, which was a blessing.

Maz enjoyed kitchen duty, especially food preparation. He enjoyed chopping vegetables and fruits, slicing meats, and all the chores needed to get a meal ready to cook on the open fires. Bread making was enjoyable, too. Maz was sure that by the time he finished at the University he would be able to cook his own meals. That would save a lot of money! The University food was good, and his mother's cooking was even better. He knew, however, that someday he would be assigned somewhere far from his mother's kitchen, and he should learn to fend for himself. It would make him more desirable as a partner, also, he thought smugly. Cleaning ability would be appreciated, too. They said the women in the Bloody Mountains chose their husbands primarily for their cleaning and cooking abilities. Of course, the women of the Highlands and Spine favored good hunters, and the southern women liked warriors. Northern women looked for good fishermen. It was confusing, but he had already made up his mind to learn as much as possible.

When the cleaning was done and the streets in good order, he returned to his parents' home. The five domes were as familiar to him as his own hand, and spoke to him of comfort and care. He knew his mother and father would both be home by now, getting ready for the winter solstice festivities. Uncle Cree, his wife, and their daughters would be there, as would Lupo and Tahari. A family gathering, which was appropriate. He knew there would be the traditional foods; squash soup, cakes with winter berries, loaves of bread with chunks of fruit, smoked meats and fish, boiled beans, grilled maize and pie, lots of pie. There would be mead, of course, and spiced wine. Tall cups of water with pieces of fruit for flavor. Hot tea with spices and honey. Everything he could want.

There would be singing; all the traditional songs he knew from his childhood, and some Ryzen favorites. They would play games. He knew his mother would insist he put his boots outside the door for Old Woman Winter to leave him gifts. Obviously, it was his parents who procured the gifts, but they enjoyed the pretense. It was his favorite time of year. He had prepared presents for the family gift exchange, and half the fun was seeing if they could figure out the identity of the giver, who was supposed to make the gifts secretly by hand. He had made beaded bracelets for the women and necklaces for the men, using skills he learned in the Academy. He had a special gift for Lupo, too. He was giving him his own knife, the one Draq had made; he kept Draq's knife, which he had used to balance the scales. He wished he could do more complicated arts, but beading and drawing were all he could do. He thought someday he might like to become a smith; then he could learn to make swords and knives, like his brother had done. Being a Ryzen was all he had ever wanted, but it meant that being the best Ryzen he could be was his primary focus and training, above all other interests, including a wife and making knives. There would be time for that later, Someday.

The tables were laden with food, as they had been at the wedding last season. The scent of winter spices was in the air. His mother had purchased the smoked meats, and he realized he was hungry. Before the food, however, they would sing.

He got a cup of tea just in time. His aunt sounded the first note, and everyone joined in. The first song was an ode to winter.

Snowflakes falling on the ground,

Happy children all around.

See the pine cones I have found;

Winter is a-coming!

Jolly women singing songs;

Husbands, won't you sing along?

Brothers, sisters, sing out strong;

Winter is a-coming!

Take a cup of winter cheer,

Only friends are singing here,

Be at ease and have no fear;

Winter is a-coming!

Fine the fire, full and bright;

Fine the snow in morning light.

Sing the song with all your might,

Winter is a-coming!

Here is food and here is fire,

Here is music on the lyre.

Here our happy songs inspire.

Winter is a-coming!

Turn your frowns all upside down,

Dancing, prancing all around,

Only joyfulness abound,

Winter is a-coming!

Everyone applauded as they finished the song. Then Tahari began a ballad, and they all sang that too, with men and women alternating lines. It was a question song, very popular with young people.

Who is the lad who holds my heart?

Lady, is it I?

Who is the one who holds my joy?

Lady, surely I?

Who is the one who makes me smile?

I know it is I.

Who is the one I long to know?

Lady, it is I!

Who is the one I'm looking for?

Can it then be I?

Who makes me happy every day?

Oh, I know 'tis I!

Who brings me gold and shells and iron?

Lady, it's not I.

Who fills my hands with everything?

Lady, no, not I.

Who hunts and brings me winter meat?

Sorry, 'tis not I.

Who builds me a sturdy boat?

No, no, no, not I.

Who loves me and counts not the cost?

No, oh no, not I.

Who will give everything he owns?

Certainly not I.

Who wants riches from my hand?

Lady, it is I!

Who wants clothing, fine and fair?

Lady, surely I!

Who is the selfish, greedy one?

I fear it may be I.

Get you gone, you foolish man!

Yes, my lady, aye.

By the time this song ended, they were all laughing. Then it was time for the gift exchange. Gifts were hidden all over the house, and the men had to go find them and put them in a pile in the main room. The gifts were all wrapped in sheets of fiber made from leaves. Then the women looked at them, called out the name written on the fiber wrapping, and gave it to the person. Some gifts were funny, and some gifts were sweet. They took turns opening gifts, and as each one was opened they had to guess the identity of the giver.

Maz received a cleaning cloth to polish his Ichak; that must be from Lupo! He was always after him to polish his staff. He was right, and Lupo said it would be useful in the coming seasons. A new dress tunic; he guessed his mother, and he was right. That was easy. Then he opened a package containing an atlatl, a throwing device from the southern regions. He looked around; who would give him a weapon? And a southern weapon, at that? Then he remembered Cree had been working on postings to new assignments. Would he be posted to the south? He looked, and saw a slight smile on his uncle's face. He guessed, and was right; the atlatl was from Cree.

Other gifts included gaming pieces, from his cousins; and a book, a newly leatherbound copy of the Tome of Ryzen, from his father. Quite a gift! He thanked everyone, and received thanks in turn for his beaded gifts. Lupo was touched by the gift of Maz's knife; he put it carefully in his belt, smiling. Maz went to him and grasped Lupo's forearm. "I lost one brother, but I have gained a new one." Lupo in silence gave Maz a look of understanding and gratitude. No words seemed adequate or necessary. It had been a long road since that day at the testing center. They shared a hug and the family smiled and chered.

Gratitude was the theme of the solstice, the shortest day of the year, and the theme had certainly been met this year.

Almost unnoticed in the celebration, Tahari and Wela approached Bahi, and the three of them stepped out on the balcony for private conversation. Maz, however, noticed, and crept up to the doorway to eavesdrop, a practice of most younger brothers.

It was what he had expected to hear. Tahari and Wela were asking Bahi to accept them as healer apprentices in her training program. Wela had learned the care and maintenance of livestock, but she had always been interested in healing people; Tahari had been passionately interested in healing ever since watching the healers work when she was in the healer hall after the battle. Maz was pleased. He slipped away quietly before they realized he had overheard, thinking to himself that it would be good to have a couple more healers in the family.

The celebration continued. Gradually, they all drifted into private conversations. Maz enjoyed telling his cousins about the life of a Ryzen, Tahari chatted with her mother and cousin, and Tamu was explaining his new discovery to Cree and Lupo.

"I've measured, and the object is definitely coming closer. I can't see what it actually looks like, but it reflects the light of nearby stars, so I expect it's like many of the other objects in the heavens. It doesn't give off light of its own. I don't understand the process, but I know that some objects, like the stars, produce light because of the fires within them, and others merely reflect light, like the planets."

"What about the moon?" asked Lupo.

"It's certain the moon reflects light. Yes, There are differences of opinion among scholars. Some, like the ancient sage Ra Nam, claimed the moon creates its own light from its intrinsic energy, and that energy changes throughout a month, waxing and waning, creating the darkness on the moon; but other mor learned, like Gilo Sa and myself, believe it reflects the light of the sun, and the shadow of the earth as it moves. That is what creates its phases. There have been many scrolls written on the subject. The most ancient follow the reflection theory, whereas…"

"Stop, brother! That's enough! I appreciate your vast knowledge, but there's just so much my old brain can take. I'm just a simple farmer…" Cree said, raising his hands as if in surrender.

Tamu laughed. "I've heard that 'simple farmer' excuse for years. I didn't believe it when we were young and I don't believe it now. There's nothing simple about you, brother."

Lupo grinned. "I have to agree with the Professor, sir. A simple farmer doesn't become a Guardian, or a War Chief. Let's just say you have many skills."

"And the study of the stars is not one of them," Cree said.

"I'm happy to let my brother uphold the family honor in that field of study."

"Will this object come close to the earth?" asked Lupo. "Will we be able to see it without your special lens?"

"I don't know, son. That would be exciting, but it's too soon to tell. I would like it to come close enough for us to get a good look at it, but not too close."

"Why not too close, sir?"

"Because it could cause all sorts of disturbances. The moon affects tides, and so might this object. It could change the weather and cause storms. It's better if it stays away."

"But it could happen, couldn't it?"

"Of course it could happen, son. Anything is theoretically possible. It's not likely, however, or we would see evidence of it having happened in the past." Tamu sounded sure of himself, almost obnoxiously so.

Lupo looked at Cree. Cree raised an eyebrow. He started to speak, then stopped and shook his head.

"What?" Tamu said. "Is there something I should know?"

"Not at all, brother," said Cree. "Just some old Ryzen legends. I don't think they have anything to do with the current situation." He looked meaningfully at Lupo, who shut his mouth. Lupo had heard the legends, too.

"Good. You had me worried. If there had been large scale destruction before, that would mean it might happen again. But we know the scientific maxim that what has happened before is likely to happen again, and what has not happened is not likely to happen. Meshuga's Law, I think it's called. Well, I'll go get something else to eat while there's still some left!" Tamu walked off, happy to be surrounded by his family. Cree watched him, thinking that his brother's unfailing positivity could cause problems someday.

"I think I want more to drink", said Lupo.

"That sounds good," said Cree. They walked to the table that was loaded with bowls of fruit cut into large chunks. Lupo took a piece of an orange, squeezed it, and put the piece in his water, then went to fill his cup from the water jug. Cree filled his cup first, then grabbed a large chunk of pineapple, a treat brought in by a Ryzen Sikka relay from the Western Islands. He dropped the chunk into his cup...

...and the water splashed out, overflowing, as it was displaced by the fruit. Cree looked at the glass, his mind's eye seeing oceans overflowing on the land, and thought to himself: what if the prophecy and the object Tamu was speaking of are connected?

End of Book One

Glossary

(Roughly in order of appearance.)

Ryzen: an order of warrior sages, who preserve ancient knowledge The rebuilders of the world and protectors the people of Timur Laut and the seven realms.

Wailu kile: a mineral that can be used as an energy source to power vehicles and weapons, and probably many other applications. Much knowledge was lost.

Banua Zalagi: the land and people of the southeast region of Timur Laut.

Timur Laut: the northwest continent and some of the adjacent islands off the western coast

Tambak Citadel: capital of Timur Laut, the northeastern peninsula of the continent.

Maga Vihar: University, college, any higher learning institute

Vihar: generic for school

Alaya: house

Aiglu: the dome shaped structures used for rooms in the alayas of Timur Laut, typically made of stone in colder climates and clay in warm climates.

Falu pau: a dining hall or restaurant

Vatiga Rishi: engineer, technician, highly skilled mechanic or scientist, especially skilled in metallurgy

Hokulani: wayfinder

Rishiken: technology, old learning

Vidura: Collected sayings

Hokulan: wayfinding

Lana: an outdoor living area adjacent to a house

Nine Grandmothers: the ruling council of Timur Laut

Makarishi: another title for the Nine Grandmothers

Yudansha Rishi: the Sages, the Black vests of the Ryzen

Capaicha: helmet that links the mind of a Ryzen to his ichak and sikka

Ichak: the ancient weapon of the Ryzen, a staff with energy powers.

Sikka: the three-passenger flying craft of the Ryzen. Plural is Sikka Manu.

Theralonia: a large island between the northwest and northeast continents

Nesos City: capital of Theralonia

Continents: Four main continents, the northwest, northeast, southwest, and southeast. There are two islands in between the northern and southern continental masses, Theralonia to the north, and Kukabura to the south. Small islands dot the fringes of the continents. The earth's surface at the time of the story is two thirds land, one third water.

Tenifra: the southwest coast of the northeastern continent

Guayota Cor: largest city in Tenifra, one of the largest on the northeastern continent.

Pixos: a unit of measure, about half a meter in length. Roughly the length of the average man's forearm from elbow to middle fingertip (18-20 inches).

People

MazKawa Kau, young man who wants to be a Ryzen, youngest child of Tamu and Bahi Kau.

Tamu Kau, a Professor of Star Science at the University of Timur Laut, the Maga Vihar

Bahi Kau, a professor of Healing Arts at the Maga Vihar, wife of Tamu Kau, mother of Maz, Draq (Draraq) Kau, son of Bahi and Tamu, brother of Maz. Draq is a Vatiga Rishi, a specialist in metals

Tahari Kau, daughter of Tamu and Bahi, sister to Maz and Draq.Tahari is a teacher of young children.

CreeVa Kau, (or just Cree), brother of Tamu Kau, Ryzen, Craftmaster of the Farmers' Guild, later War Chief and Guardian of Timur Laut,

Mahani Kau, Farmer and Herbseller/healer, Ryzen, keeper of healing lore, wife of Cree Kau

Yani Kau, weaver apprentice, daughter of Cree Kau and Mahani Kau

Wela Kau, livestock apprentice and (later) healer apprentice, daughter of Cree Kau and Mahani Kau

Lupo Kai, Ryzen pilot and wayfinder, Blue Feather and training crew chief for Maz.

Kal Namu, Ryzen pilot

Dom Morro, villager, wrestler, later Ryzen classmate of Maz

Matay, senior Ryzen ambassador to Theralonia

ChoGun Miya, A Ryzen sage in the cadre of sages

Brakos, rogue Theralonian Senator, promoter of war

Agricolos, Delegate in Theralonian Assembly

Improbos, Delegate in Theralonian Assembly

Miros, former guardsman of Brakos, who turns against him.

Stoltos, guardsman of Brakos

Dimas, guardsman of Brakos

Stercos, guardsman of Brakos

Degos, guardsman of Brakos

Kanos, guardsman of Brakos

Dynasis, guardsman of Brakos

About the Author

J.D. Warburton is the pen name of a mother-son writing team.

John Cofer is a Navy vetran and a black belt Brazilian Jiu Jitsu instructor, teaching his own group of "Ryzen" in the Pacific Northwest, where he lives with his lovely lady, daughter, and grandkids.

Therese Martin is a retired history teacher who also writes historical novels as Therese Martin, and young adult science fiction as Terry Martin. She lives in the Pacific Northwest with her husband and a plethora of descendants.

Summary

18 year old Maz was finished with his schooling, and it was time to take that first step towards his lifelong dream of becoming a Ryzen. The Ryzen were "the best of the best", guardians of the ancient knowledge, protectors of the nation of Timur Laut. He had wanted to join their ranks since childhood. He was certain he would be accepted; all his life, he had succeeded at everything he attempted.

But not this time. After a painful rejection, he goes to train with his uncle Cree, a "retired" Ryzen. Hard lessons follow, along with grievous loss and the threat of war. Can Maz learn the ways of a warrior in time? Will he fight to protect his homeland? And what's the nameless threat the Grandmothers have prophesied, that could destroy not only Timur Laut, but the entire world?

The New Recruit is the first book in the Ryzen Saga, from the days before catastrophe changed the world...